Academic Life
in
Sixteen
10-Minute Plays

David K. Farkas

Dedication

To Jonah and Hazel and to all the dedicated teachers they have had and will have as they grow older.

Acknowledgments

Susan and Charles Blank, Robert Caston, Jean Farkas, Marty Levine, Josh Mendel, Roy E. Schreiber, and Myron Tuman provided astute and creative suggestions on this manuscript and talked me out of some of my worst ideas. Ziaul Haque contributed his expertise in graphic design, book design, and digital publishing.

Credits

I shot the photographs that appear on the front and back cover of this book. They show Loew Hall, on the University of Washington campus. A big chunk of my life was spent in that building.

Table of Contents

Introduction

I am a creature of schools. I started nursery school at age 4, and until I transitioned to emeritus status (retirement) in 2014, I never failed to heed the ringing of the school bell each fall. I went straight from high school (Clifton, New Jersey), to college (University of Rochester), then to graduate school (the University of Chicago and the University of Minnesota), and then to three successive faculty positions: Texas Tech University, West Virginia University, and, for most of my career, the University of Washington. I've had close contact with other colleges and universities as well.

My degrees are all in English literature. My plan, from early on, was to become an English professor. When I began graduate school, new Ph.D.s could readily find good faculty positions. If you had specialized in Romantic poetry, that's the kind of job you could get. However, I watched the academic job market deteriorate each year I was in graduate school, and when I finished, jobs for new Ph.D.'s had nearly evaporated. For all of us Ph.D. students, the situation was disastrous. Some took low-paying jobs in bookstores and the like, deeply disappointing not just themselves but their entire families. One turned to alcohol. Another—a handsome fellow—was divorced by his wife and moved to Japan to start a career in modeling. One female Ph.D. student became a bank robber and successfully robbed several banks before she was caught. I fell farther than the rest. I strayed from the humanities to become a teacher in the deeply disdained field of technical writing. Here was a specialty in which faculty positions were readily available, even if—like me—you had minimal credentials. When word got out among the graduate students that I'd gotten a job teaching technical writing, few envied me.

The cultural divide between science and the humanities is large, as C. P. Snow pointed out long ago *(The Two Cultures, 1959)*. In academia, this takes the form of mutual suspicion and distaste between the humanities and career-focused fields such as engineering and business. The various social science and natural science departments fall somewhere in the middle of this divide. This divide has played a large role in my professional life.

Engineers tend to regard the humanities faculty as irrelevant to the modern world, providers of useless courses for dilettantes. Humanities folks, in return, often regard engineering faculty as half-educated servants of evil corporations. Engineering and most other applied fields bring in government research funding and reap corporate largess. Teaching loads are lighter. Offices are spiffy. Salaries are high. Humanities departments just hobble along. In one English department I taught in, getting to use the photocopier was a luxury. There was no supply cabinet where you could grab paper clips or a yellow notepad.

To engineering faculty, a teacher of writing, even technical writing, is a humanities person. Beyond this, you are often a serious impediment to their curriculum. Engineering departments want to pack as many technical courses as possible into their students' course of study. Only grudgingly, and to meet engineering accreditation standards, do they leave a space in the curriculum for a technical writing course.

Nor do engineering faculty much respect us as professionals: "What kind of research can you tech comm folks do? Everything's already been written down in grammar books." Engineers have difficulty appreciating research that doesn't contain numbers. When you teach technical communication, even praise can be painful, as when the chair of an engineering department told me, "I'm glad my students are taking your technical writing course instead of that Shakespeare shit." To be fair, most engineering chairs would simply lament that their students' course of study is simply too crowded to permit much in the way of humanities electives.

English department faculty generally have no fondness for the technical writing courses that their department may reluctantly offer. To them, this is the dirty, corrupt part of the world pushing its way through their door. It is worse when enrollments in literature courses are reduced because a technical writing course can be counted as a humanities elective. So, the academic version of the Snow's Two Cultures Divide often leaves technical writing faculty with no friends at all.

This tension between the humanities and applied fields can be seen in Vice Provost Sherman's swipe at the English department in "Tenure Denied" and in the central administration's shabby treatment of humanities faculty in "Travel Money." It is on full display in "The Special Status of Clara de Jong," where a provost who comes from the business school scoffs at the humanities, and an English department chair responds sharply.

I stand in the middle of this divide. I wish I could wholeheartedly subscribe to the claim that a humanities education prepares a young person for career success as a generalist. On the other hand, I deeply believe that all students should have a meaningful education in the humanities, even if this means extending certain undergraduate degree programs to five years.

Having jumped into technical communication knowing nothing about it, I worked hard to learn my new field. Soon I found that I liked it. I was raised in a business-friendly family, and I do not have a reflexive hostility toward corporations. Also, I was curious about such fields as petroleum engineering and wildlife biology, and I examined my students' assignments with interest. As time went on, I got to teach students who were majoring in technical communication and ultimately teach tech communication graduate students.

There were, however, those distressing times when our department—having no strong allies or defenders—went on the chopping block for elimination—and narrowly escaped. Across the United States, even the best technical communication departments and programs are eliminated or greatly scaled back with disturbing frequency. My old department is now gone. If you detect some edginess in these plays, it comes in part from having devoted my career to a singularly unloved and precarious corner of the academic world.

A related but different tension in the academic world pervades these plays: the corporate university vs. the traditional, knowledge-driven university. The corporate university prioritizes efficiency, measurement of anything that can be measured, and top-down control of instruction. In addition, it seeks out any and all sources of funding. This tension is not new. As far back as 1915, Thorstein Veblen condemned North American universities for surrendering to the business world and adopting managerial values and practices (*The Higher Learning in America: A Memorandum on the Conduct of Universities by Business Men*).

This tension stands out in four of the plays. Professor Eric Sloane's insistence on autonomy in the classroom is the driving issue in "Quality Work." The pressure on faculty to secure research funding and to prioritize research with commercial possibilities is treated satirically in "Stripes" and grimly in "Tenure Denied." In "Wasserman the Water Man," a corporate donor pressures a department chair to squelch a student's research project because it reveals high levels of pollutants in a local river. In contrast, the ideals of the knowledge-driven university shine forth in "Echoes of the Professor" and in "Margaret Reynolds Enters Heaven." My biases are not hidden. Reading these plays, you will surely notice that faculty members are generally good guys, and deans and provosts are the bad guys. Department chairs who align themselves with their faculty are good. Chairs who are co-opted by higher-level administrators do not come off well.

Surely I am being unfair. There are very decent provosts and deans. But my main goal is always to tell engrossing stories about people, and to do this, especially in very brief plays, I needed to create a more concentrated version of the world I actually see around me. Think about Western movies. In Westerns, you are not likely to find sweet-tempered cattle barons or kindly men who are pushing through a railroad. The world of the Western movie is made simpler and more extreme in order to make good stories possible. I have done the same. Furthermore, many of the plays in this collection are entirely personal stories and have nothing to do with the tensions that pervade university life.

Finally, a word about how this collection came together. From my 80-plus 10-minute plays, I selected those that dealt with universities. Then I let my imagination loose on the academic world and wrote "Quality Work," "Travel Money," "Academic Misconduct," "Navigation Problem," "Tenure Denied," and "The Special Status of Clara de Jong." Then I sequenced the plays and wrote the postscripts, this introduction, and an afterword. This is the same procedure I used previously to put together my collection, *Fourteen Jewish Flavored 10-Minute Plays.* The *Academic Life* collection actually consists of seventeen plays rather than the sixteen stated in the book's title. This is because "Wasserman the Water Man" previously appeared in *Fourteen Jewish Flavored 10-Minutes Plays* and "Echoes of the Professor," previously appeared in *Performing 10-Minute Plays with Friends,* a how-to book that includes ten 10-minute plays that I've placed in the public domain. So, if you have read one of the other books, you will still have 16 new plays to read in this collection.

Paradise in Tennessee

A 10-minute play by

David K. Farkas

Setting:

It is 1971. The play begins in a basement corridor of a classroom building on the University of Minnesota campus.

Characters:

Paul Rogers: Assistant Professor, Department of English, University of Minnesota.

Jim Thompson: An undergraduate, but perhaps in his mid-20s. He is a member of the radical student organization SDS, Students for a Democratic Society.

Josh: A graduate student in history. He is in his 30's and is president of the SDS chapter at the University of Minnesota.

FBI Agent 1

FBI Agent 2

Suggested minimum casting:

Paul Rogers

Jim Thompson/FBI Agent

Josh/FBI Agent

[Scene 1]

    THOMPSON accosts ROGERS.

THOMPSON: Hey, motherfucker!

    ROGERS is startled.

THOMPSON: Hey, you. Rogers. Motherfucker.

ROGERS: What?

THOMPSON: Nice to see you again . . . "Pro-fess-or Rogers."

ROGERS: You're Jim Thompson.

THOMPSON: I'm "Uhuru Thompson" now. Got that, Motherfucker?

ROGERS: You were in my Romantic poetry course. For about 5 weeks, as I remember. I think I'll be moving along, Mr. Thompson.

    THOMPSON takes a handgun from his jacket.

THOMPSON: You're not going anywhere. As a matter of fact, you may have reached the end of the line. I remembered that you like to use the basement door. I can put a bullet through you, walk out the door, and be gone. Someone might hear the shot—or not. Good chance the janitor will find you sometime tonight.

ROGERS: Why me? Why this?

THOMPSON: Cause you're an enemy of the people. A capitalist exploiter of the working class.

ROGERS: I've done nothing to you. I've done nothing at all. And I'm not much of a capitalist. I get a salary like everyone else.

THOMPSON: A fat salary! You're just a pawn for the Man. What's your Ph.D.? Just a ticket into the ruling class. What's your literary culture? Just another way to draw class distinctions. I'm not in that game anymore. *(Gestures to the gun.)* I bet you've never seen one of these before. Not close up.

ROGERS: Not pointed straight at me. But I was in the Reserves. We didn't do much with sidearms, but I've handled guns like that.

THOMPSON: Reserves? You shot some of those students at Kent State? Today is payback. *(Gestures threateningly with the gun.)*

ROGERS: *(Showing real fear.)* I was nowhere near Kent State. My active service was five years ago, and—actually—it was pretty relaxed.

THOMPSON: What if you *had* been there? What if your superior officer had shouted an order, "Kill the students. Kill as many as you can." What would you have done?

ROGERS: I'd like to think I would have refused. Refused and told others to refuse. But I can't tell you what I'd have done. I don't know.

THOMPSON: You would have followed orders and shot. Then kept on shooting.

ROGERS: I'll never know. That's the honest answer for you.

THOMPSON: You didn't join the student walkout. You're teaching your classes like nothing is happening. Nixon is bombing Cambodia. Black prisoners were killed for no reason at Attica. And you just want to keep lecturing about Romantic poetry!

ROGERS: Almost nobody on the faculty has joined the walkout. The English department is giving incompletes so that students who walk out can finish their courses when they choose to.

THOMPSON: You think that's enough, Professor Rogers? It's not. I'm giving you one chance. Cancel your classes and join the walkout. Announce it at the beginning of your next class and send them all out the door.

ROGERS: I'll cancel. I promise. Tuesday morning. Ten o'clock class.

THOMPSON: I know—Tuesday. I'll be waiting.

> THOMPSON bolts offstage. ROGERS almost collapses from the
> tension he was under, but recovers.

[Scene 2]

> JOSH sits in a thrift-store chair, possibly an old office chair. He wears
> a Che Guevara T-shirt. He is speaking on a midcentury landline
> phone that is on the floor or else on a battered desk. Other set items
> may suggest the make-shift office of a campus SDS chapter.

JOSH: I don't know anything about this . . . Yes, he's a member—sort of. Or maybe he isn't a member. I don't really know. I don't have to tell you shit.

> Listens attentively.

JOSH: Yes . . . No . . . I don't . . . Today? Right now? I don't need you ordering me around. You get that?

> Listens attentively, showing more accommodation.

JOSH: OK. Riverbend Park. Near the bridge. One hour . . . No police! Yes. Yes. We'll talk.

[Scene 3]

> A park bench with ROGERS and JOSH seated. At some point one of the characters may stand.

ROGERS: I didn't have to phone you. I could have just called the police. They could have protected me—and my family—and picked up Thompson in short order. He's no criminal mastermind.

JOSH: Don't make such a big deal out of all this. He was probably just trying to scare you. You don't know if the gun was loaded. You don't even know if it was a real gun.

ROGERS: It was a real gun. I was there, and you weren't. Maybe his plan was just to scare me—and he sure did that. But I have no reason to think he didn't have bullets in that gun. And I don't think he had a plan. When he found me, he didn't know whether he'd shoot me or not.

JOSH: Well, he isn't Mr. Mental Stability.

ROGERS: By not calling the police, I'm taking a huge chance. He could be threatening someone else with that gun—right now. He could have just shot someone this exact minute. I'd be morally responsible. Maybe legally responsible, for not calling the police immediately. Do you get this?

JOSH: Yes.

ROGERS: Do you get that you're responsible now too? Just like me. When I phoned you, you made the same decision not to call the police. You might say we're in this together.

JOSH: Yes, I understand. It's good that you phoned me. I wouldn't want to see him arrested. The police would probably beat the crap out of him. Some judge would send him to jail for 20 years. The things he wants are the right things. He's just not disciplined.

ROGERS: Definitely "not disciplined." So, do you have a plan? I assume you can find him—and get the gun away from him.

JOSH: Yes, we can do that. There's not that many places he would be, and we can talk to him, "influence" him. He's the kind of person who can be "influenced."

ROGERS: OK. After you've "influenced" the gun away from him, then what? What are you going to do? How do you know he won't get another gun? Do something else crazy and dangerous? This is now more your show than mine. Do you have a plan?

JOSH: Yes, I have a plan. There's a place in Tennessee—a commune. Driving hard, you can get there in a day or so. People at "the Farm" are gentle, caring. But in their own way, they're strict. Anything Jim does, they'll know about it. It's way out in the hills. If Jim even started to leave, they'd know. They'd know, and I'd know. But he's not going to want to leave. It's a great place. He'll be glad to go there, and he'll be glad to stay. Maybe for years. Maybe he'll get his head cleaned out.

ROGERS: What? SDS has a sanitorium for its deranged members?

JOSH: The Farm isn't related to SDS. These are people I know. There is no division between rich and poor. They are self-sufficient, raise almost all their own food. It's not small. They have members who are doctors. They have their own little clinic. They do some health care for poor folks who live nearby. They've gotten some acceptance from the locals.

ROGERS: Somehow I don't quite see Jim Thompson toiling in the fields or baking bread or doing anything else useful.

JOSH: Useful comes later. But, he'll stay. It's beautiful there. It's "spiritual"—for those who want that. They have some really fine musicians. Lots of pot and drugs—but in a good way, a healthy way. Oh, it's a "free love" community.

ROGERS exhibits interest in this idea.

JOSH: They've moved beyond all the dysfunctions of traditional relationships. Men no longer "own" their women. The women insist on equality and sexual freedom.

ROGERS: Yes, of course. Very enlightened ideas. Shit! Why aren't you there? Why can't I be there? Jim Thompson gets all this for pointing a gun to my stomach!

JOSH: I visit. And I *work* when I visit. But I never stay for long. I'm committed to the struggle of the Proletariat. That mostly means cities, not some commune. Also, I'm a doctoral student in history—labor history. But I want my scholarship to really speak to people, so I'm looking to find my voice. For me, that's a city thing.

ROGERS: I understand. But the Farm does sound very special.

JOSH: Yes, the Farm and places like it are one path into the future. Just not my path. *(Laughing.)* I don't think it's much of a path for you either. I'd sure like to be there when you showed up. "You all looking for a professor of Romantic poetry? I can tell you all you want to know about Blake and Wordsworth. I'll give lectures by the campfire in the evenings. All I need is a nice cabin and some of that free love."

ROGERS: *(Laughing.)* Is that asking for too much?

The JOSH points to ROGERS' wedding ring.

JOSH: I couldn't say. You'd have to ask Mrs. Rogers about the free love part.

ROGERS: Maybe I could interest Louise in the free love part! You don't know till you ask. William Blake believed in free love. He would have joined the Farm in a second. Mrs. Blake would have been happy baking in the communal kitchen.

JOSH: I think you've gone off your rocker. You might have caught it from Thompson. Are you forgetting? This is actually a very serious discussion—or it was. And we're not exactly friends, not exactly on the same side.

ROGERS: OK. We're not exactly friends, but we do seem able to relate to each other. And, yes, this is a very serious discussion. For one thing, I do believe I almost got killed this afternoon. But . . . *(Laughing.)* I have a sabbatical coming up! I can explain to my chair, "I'll be in Tennessee studying the cultural milieu of the paradisal vision of the Romantic Movement." I won't mention the social arrangements.

JOSH starts warming up to the subject.

JOSH: *(Laughing.)* Yes. Yes. You and Jim Thompson will be buddies. You'll entertain everyone with the story of how he pointed a pistol at you. Someone might write it up as a folk song, a talking blues. The "Nearly Shot My Professor Talking Blues." It would go over well at one of the evening songfests. When the singing is over, the men look for a willing woman, the women look for a suitable man, and the couples slip off to their cabins.

ROGERS: This sounds better and better. I can even bake bread, if that's what they want. Jim and I will become great friends. We'll always be glad to see you when you find the time to visit.

ROGERS makes a move as though to leave.

ROGERS: Time to get back to reality. I told Louise I needed to stay late on campus, but it's definitely time for me to get home.

They both stand and face each other. There is warmth between them.

JOSH: You know, Rogers. I think you're a decent guy. More than that. I'm thinking we can trust each other.

ROGERS: I don't know that I ever didn't trust you.

JOSH: *(Laughing.)* Well, Professor "Running Dog of the Imperialist Warmongers," I definitely distrusted you at first. But not now. You know, I can envision us meeting again some time. Or, talking on the phone.

ROGERS: Sure.

JOSH: I mean for a reason—a serious reason . . . There might be situations . . . up ahead . . . when I'd need to communicate, very privately, with the University administration. I'm sure not going to contact them directly. But if I gave you a message, you—a professor— could talk to them, and they'd believe it was solid information that came from SDS. Not just a crazy story.

ROGERS: OK. Like what kind of message?

JOSH: Like maybe a warning about something. There are SDS people who are more extreme than us. The Wisconsin group. Other people from out of state. I'll always be loyal to them. But . . . stuff might happen. Bad stuff . . . Are you going to tell your wife about this meeting? I'm asking you not to.

ROGERS: I really could. She'd be totally discrete. But, I don't need her knowing that I could have died today. So, I won't tell her anything. This is just between you and me.

JOSH: Thanks, Paul.

JOSH exits.

[Scene 4]

ROGERS is seated in the classic "interrogation chair" with two FBI agents. He is wearing different clothing than in the last scene.

AGENT 1: You're half-way to being a hero, Professor Rogers. You did prevent a significant loss of life. But you're only half a hero, and the other half of the equation is equally important.

AGENT 2: We do not believe that someone just walked up to you and told you a campus building would be blown up. The only reason we emptied twenty buildings is that we didn't regard this as one more random bomb scare. When you spoke to the provost, you indicated that you had direct information . . .

ROGERS: That's an exaggeration!

AGENT 2: No, it is not. You know something about who did the bombing, and you need to tell us.

AGENT 1: If you'd come clean in the first place, maybe we could have stopped the bombing from happening. But we understand that you were completely focused on preventing loss of life. Not much interest in the destruction of a building. *(Showing contempt.)* Sort of a professor's way of looking at things.

AGENT 2: We think you want to tell us right now, except that you're afraid of SDS. We can protect you from them.

ROGERS: No. I was walking on College Avenue. Some guy—I *hardly* saw him—stepped up behind me, warned me about the bombing, and slipped away. That's what happened.

AGENT 1: Refusing to tell us the truth makes you an accessory to a felony—a major felony. That's a lot of jail time, Professor.

AGENT 2: What if there's another bombing? And people are killed? Do you want to be responsible for that?

ROGERS: You've heard my answer.

AGENT 1: We are going to connect you to the bombing or to people who knew about it. We're interrogating everyone. We'll find things out.

Maybe we'll give someone a chance to get off easier by giving you up. One way or another, we're going to get the evidence we need.

AGENT 2: You have exactly one chance, Professor Rogers, and it's now.

ROGERS: I've told you the exact truth, and I'm guilty of nothing.

AGENT 1: That may be true for right now, Professor Rogers. You can go home. But, we're not done with you.

[Scene 5]

> On one side of the stage we see ROGERS standing against a dirty wall on which there's a pay phone. The clothes he was wearing in the previous scene are now disheveled. He is furtive and nervous.

ROGERS: Louise, listen. Don't say a word. I need to hang up in maybe 30 seconds. I got picked up by the FBI. They have an idea that I'm connected to the bombing, that I have information. Yes, I know . . . crazy. But there are things that make them suspicious—some students I know. Some other stuff, and they're not letting go of this. I'm at a Trailways station . . . No, not in Minnesota. There's someone I need to talk with. Find out where this is going. What I should do next. The FBI may be listening on your line, maybe trying to trace this call. I love you, Louise.

> He hangs up and exits hurriedly.

[Scene 6]

> JOSH and JIM are in a room with a simple rustic table and a chair or two. There is one place at the table set with a bowl, a mug, and some utensils.

JOSH: *(Looking at his watch.)* He's still not up?

THOMPSON: No. When Sheila and Tex met up with him, he was exhausted and a complete wreck. They took him to a cottage, and he just crashed . . . Oh, I think I hear him coming up the walk.

> ROGERS enters. THOMPSON hugs him.

THOMPSON: Welcome, Professor Rogers. You'll be safe here. You gave me a big break, and we're all here for you now. You can stay for as long as you like.

JOSH: It's good to see you, Paul. So, here you are in Tennessee! Here we are, the three of us, all together in that paradise you were hankering for.

ROGERS: But not quite the circumstances I was dreaming about.

THOMPSON: You'll like it here, Professor Rogers. For me, it's changed everything. We are going to transform the whole world—but not by revolution. We are doing it by example, every day. If you don't mind giving up your fancy professorship, you can join us.

ROGERS: Thanks, Jim. But I'm hoping this will just be a quick visit.

JOSH: My situation is sticky. They're not going to give up trying to connect the head of the SDS chapter to the bombing. And there *are* connections. It's likely I'll need to stay hidden here for a long time— maybe for years. But, Paul, you can go home. Whatever happens to me, you're safe with the story you told the FBI. Not one of the Wisconsin people knows anything about you.

ROGERS: Thank you, Josh . . . There's a bond between us that will never be broken.

THOMPSON: *(Laughing.)* We have our bond too!

> THOMPSON pantomimes holding a pistol to ROGERS and then grows serious.

THOMPSON: I'll always be grateful to you . . . Whenever you're ready, we'll drive you back to Minneapolis. No one will know you were ever here with us.

> ROGERS nods. Then turns to JOSH.

ROGERS: Josh, what are you going to do here? What about your dissertation?

JOSH: I guess my dissertation is on hold. But it's a sacrifice I'm prepared to make. Many people have willingly given their lives fighting for a better future. I can give up my academic plans.

ROGERS: But maybe that won't be necessary. It won't be simple, but I have friends at a dozen universities. If we're careful, we can get you the books you'll need to do your writing on labor history. *(Pause.)* Or, maybe, you should write about what you've done and what you've seen. You've *become* part of the history of these crazy times, and the day will come when you can publish what you write.

JOSH: Yes! Maybe that will be my life here in Tennessee. I can explain what SDS accomplished and what we did wrong. Strategic errors we made. The Minnesota bombing and the other campus bombings can be the narrative center of what I'll write.

ROGERS: Yes. Yes. Josh, you were looking to find your voice. I think you're finding it. And, Jim, I think you've found *yourself* down here in Tennessee.

THOMPSON: I think so. And I know that living here is good for me—at least for a while. I try hard to contribute to this wonderful community that welcomed me. I try to be a good friend to everyone. I've learned to bake bread.

The End

Postscript to "Paradise in Tennessee"

Scene 1 and the first part of Scene 2 are largely factual. I studied under the professor I call "Paul Rogers," and one evening he hosted the students in his graduate seminar at his home. He told us that, just days before, he'd been threatened at gunpoint by an unstable campus radical and that he'd chosen to let the University of Minnesota SDS group handle the problem rather than contact the police.

I invented Rogers' service in the National Guard and the specifics of his conversation with the SDS leader, which I believe took place entirely by phone. And, of course, the actual SDS leader did not warn my professor about plans for a bombing on the University of Minnesota campus. There was no such bombing in Minnesota, although there was plenty of violent protesting—including the Dinkyown Uprising of 1970—with riot-squad police, tear gas, and burning automobiles.

> https://hclib.tumblr.com/post/116127500902/red-barn-occupation-the-1970-dinkytown-uprising

My own connection to the Farm is just a fleeting one. Sometime in the early 1970s, I watched a converted school bus painted with flamboyant hippie graphics roll through the University of Minnesota campus. "The Farm" was emblazoned on the side. Someone inside the bus reached out through an open window and threw me a pamphlet describing their counter-culture settlement in rural Tennessee and their plan to show the world a new and better social order. I was deeply moved by the pamphlet and imagined Jean Farkas and I joining them, although this was certainly not going to happen. Fifty years later that pamphlet came to mind as I conceived this play. Up until the moment I wrote this postscript (June 25, 2022), it had not occurred to me to find out what had become of the Farm. My assumption was that this commune, like so many others, had disappeared long ago. But, much to my delight, I find that the Farm still exists, although in a different form:

https://thefarmcommunity.com/

https://en.wikipedia.org/wiki/The_Farm_(Tennessee)

From their website, it is apparent that the residents of the Farm are interested in their early history. I will certainly send them a copy of this book. I hope they will like how they are portrayed in this play.

Echoes of the Professor

A 10-minute play by

David K. Farkas

Characters:

Sandra: A woman in her 30s. She is the daughter of Julia, who has recently died. Julia was predeceased by her husband, Nick.

Sam: Sandra's husband, also in his 30s.

Julia: Mentioned in Scene 1. In Scenes 2 and 3, which are set in 1968, she appears as a college senior, about to graduate and marry Nick.

Nick: Mentioned in Scene 1. In Scenes 2 and 3, he is a college senior about to graduate and marry Julia.

Attorney: An older man. He is settling Julia's estate.

John: In 1968, a crematorium employee, an older man.

Horace: In 1968, a long-deceased professor, an elderly man.

Suggested minimum casting:

Attorney/John/Horace

Sandra/Julia

Sam

Nick

[Scene 1]

> SAM and SANDRA, a married couple, professional in manner, are seated at a table in the law offices of the ATTORNEY, who is the executor of the estate of JULIA, SANDRA'S mother. On the table is a large, buff-colored ceramic urn.

SANDRA: *(Pointing to urn.)* So there it is. I'd sort of forgotten about the urn.

ATTORNEY: When Julia made the move to assisted living, she entrusted it to me. I could have kept the urn securely stored here in the office. That's the usual thing we do. But . . . I took it home and put it on a shelf in my living room. It certainly didn't fit the décor, but I don't entertain much anyway. Actually, "The Professor" *(Gestures toward urn.)* and I have become friends, so to speak.

SAM: Can you review the codicil for us, before we settle this issue. It's definitely puzzling.

ATTORNEY: Yes, of course. From a legal standpoint, it's entirely straightforward—and binding. And there was no question about Julia's mental competence. But Julia was disinclined to explain her reasons. *(Pause.)* Quite simply, the two of you, as a single legal entity, must choose to receive either the urn or the Chagall lithograph. If you choose the urn, I am directed to arrange for the sale of the Chagall, with the proceeds going to the United Fund. If you choose the Chagall, the urn *(Looks down at notes.)* "must be immediately disposed of as trash." This is disturbing but entirely legal in New York State. Julia was pleasant, as she always was, but very definite. I wish I could tell you more. Speaking only from a personal perspective, and especially as I've been keeping the urn myself, I'll be much happier if you choose The Professor. But, of course, giving up the Chagall would not be an entirely rational course of action. Sandra, you say that Julia . . . that Nick . . . neither one ever explained anything about the urn, even how they came by it?

SANDRA: It was just there—"The Professor"—on a shelf in our living room. It seemed important, but, no, they never explained it. Perhaps it's the ashes of a distant relative, someone they didn't know by name, but they knew he'd been a professor of something somewhere. Just once, I really pressed Mom about this. All she said was "Some things in life you need to learn on your own" . . . But how can we learn something like this?

SAM: You can see how unfortunate this situation is. We are reluctant to give up the Chagall, but it's . . . well . . . creepy to . . . you know . . . *(Gestures a tossing motion.)* to . . . ditch the urn. Of course, I'll follow Sandra's lead on this.

SANDRA: I think we need to choose the urn. It seems disrespectful to put any human remains "in the trash." And, there was clearly some kind of relationship between "The Professor" and my parents.

SAM: Yes, I guess we'll keep the urn—on a shelf in our living room, just as Julia and Nick did. Obviously, would be a lot nicer to display the Chagall lithograph.

SANDRA: I know, Sam. But, somehow The Professor just seems to belong to us. Maybe he is a distant relative, maybe not. But I know he is ours.

SAM: Maybe Marc Chagall is a distant relative. That would be a reason to pass on The Professor and keep the Chagall in our living room . . . Just joking, Sandy.

ATTORNEY: Speaking, again, as a friend rather than as your attorney, I can't help but think that there's some kind of wisdom behind your mother's final directive. Julia was always an insightful woman.

SAM: And he and Nick raised an "insightful" daughter. So, I'm good with this.

ATTORNEY: OK, we've reached a decision. So, first I'll ask Sandra to sign and initial the codicil.

> He hands SANDRA the codicil and points successively to places on the sheet of paper. She signs and initials.

ATTORNEY: And now you, Sam.

> He hands SAM the codicil and points successively to places on the sheet of paper. He too signs and initials.

ATTORNEY: Fortunately, even without the Chagall, the estate is substantial. I think that the codicil was Julia's way to make clear that there is something special about that urn. Perhaps giving up the Chagall was a kind of test—which you've passed. *(Turning to the urn.)* I guess I need my own little good-bye moment with The Professor . . . You know, sitting alone with *(Gazes at urn for a few moments.)* him in my condo, we used to chat once in a while.

> Hands SANDRA the urn.

ATTORNEY: Well, The Professor is yours now.

SANDRA takes the urn from the ATTORNEY with an air of gravity.

SANDRA: Thank you for everything. Especially, how you handled my mother's affairs after Dad died. You've been a good friend to this family for a long time.

ATTORNEY: Thank you, Sandra. You've been a loving daughter to Julia and to Nick. *(Turning to include SAM.)* And you too, Sam. You both gave them a great deal of happiness.

They all stand. SANDRA and SAM exit.

[Scene 2]

JULIA and NICK, holding hands, stroll on stage. They are dressed for spring weather. Their clothing suggests college students of an earlier time.

NICK: I had no idea we'd come out on Mt. Hope Avenue.

JULIA: Me either.

NICK: It's a big cemetery.

JULIA: And so old and beautiful! It's sort of amazing that we're finishing up four years of college, with the cemetery right next to the campus, and we never walked through it.

NICK: Well, everyone knows it's here. But it's not like "Hey, you gotta go to the cemetery!" Everyone has lots to do and think about.

As they turn a corner, NICK points to a building.

NICK: Hey, Julia. What's that?

JULIA: Sort of a little gingerbread house. Think it's part of the cemetery?

NICK: I don't know. I guess so. That chimney is pretty damn tall for a little gingerbread house. Let's take a closer look.

JULIA: Nick, I could just leave it be and head back to campus. It's been a long walk.

NICK: Oh, come on!

He leads her forward.

NICK: The door is open. Well, half-open.

JULIA: That does not qualify as an invitation, and this does not look like a place that expects visitors.

NICK: Oh, let's do it! You only live once.

> He leads her through the (imagined) half-opened door. From inside they hear the voice of JOHN, the elderly crematorium employee.

JOHN: Well, you came through the door. You might as well come all the way in.

> JOHN is seated on a chair with a small table next to it. He sets down a thick book with a serious-looking cover. He steps forward.

JOHN: Do you know what kind of building you're in?

NICK: I think that smokestack kind of gives it away. This must be a crematorium.

JOHN: That's right. It belongs to Mt. Hope Cemetery. I've been working here for 35 years. *(Pointing.)* See that? What do you suppose it is?

NICK: The oven? Far out!

JOHN: That's right. I did a burn this morning. You might have smelled a little smoke as you walked down the path.

NICK: Wow. "A burn." Too bad we missed that.

JOHN: No. If a burn had been in progress, I would have sent you away. I keep the door open for a little cool air, but out of respect for the deceased, I would not have allowed strangers to just wander in. You understand?

JULIA: Yes. Of course we do. *(Pause.)* This is a very . . . picturesque building. Beautiful tiles embedded in the brickwork. Sort of European, Swiss, or something like that.

JOHN: This crematorium is over 100 years old. It was built during the Civil War. A lot of young men were incinerated right here. The bodies were brought here from Gettysburg, Shiloh, Chancellorsville. All those places. Lot of grief when a young man dies. *(Pause.)* We have one of the very last coal-fired ovens. Now they're all gas fired. Much cheaper and cleaner. We'll be shutting down in about nine months. There will be a new modern crematorium opening offsite. Much bigger than this place. So, if you wanted to see it, you're lucky you didn't wait too much longer.

JULIA points to an urn on a high shelf.

JULIA: That's an urn. Is that where you put the ashes of the person you burned this morning?

JOHN reaches for the urn on the shelf, takes it down, and extends it for NICK and JULIA to look at.

JOHN: Oh, no. That's "The Professor." No one even makes urns like that one anymore. Long ago, The Professor was a faculty member at the University. His will specified cremation, but he wasn't married. And no family. No one ever claimed the body, so he's been here—waiting, you might say. He was here when I was hired. We don't even know his name. All I know about The Professor was what my predecessor at this job told me—and that wasn't much. The County keeps records of every death, but this particular urn got separated from the death certificate and the Cemetery's records. So, he's "The Professor." He's kept watch from that shelf for at least 50 years, and I'm his only friend. After all these years, I am probably the only living soul who knows he ever lived.

JOHN looks long at NICK and, especially, at JULIA.

JOHN: You seem like a nice young couple. From the University? And that's an engagement ring—am I right? . . . Would you like to have The Professor?

NICK: What?

JOHN: That's what I said. The Professor would be yours . . . "To have and to hold." If you're students at the University, then you have professors. Maybe you'd like to have this one.

NICK: You mean, you'd just give us the urn? The Professor, I mean.

JOHN: Under the circumstances, I believe I would. I will retire when we close down, and I could take The Professor with me. But I don't have many years left myself, and so I'd still be facing the problem of seeing to his "future," so to speak. After all these years, I'd hate to see someone just throw him into the trash. Someone who was cleaning out this building when it closes, or someone who was cleaning out my apartment after I'm gone. Someone who just sees a clay jar and has no interest in what it might be. I don't think The Professor should go into the trash. You're young. You're from the University. Take The Professor. Please.

NICK: Yes! Absolutely. An urn full of human ashes. What could be cooler than that?

JOHN looks displeased.

JOHN: He's a person. Not a conversation piece! Do you understand what I'm talking about? If you take The Professor, it's a commitment. You keep him. Wherever you go, he goes with you. You can't just decide to get rid of him—unless, of course, you find someone else who will show him proper respect.

JULIA: I think I understand you. This is a very significant decision.

NICK: Julia, maybe this isn't such a good idea. We're going to be moving around a lot in these next few years. Traveling too. Maybe this thing is too much of a burden.

JOHN: In a sense, he will be a "burden." But you'd be showing respect for a man's life. Not a person you knew, but a person nonetheless. You are truly all he has. At least, that's how it will be after I'm gone.

JULIA: Nick. Burden or not. I think we need to take The Professor. I want The Professor. Sir, I will take good care of the urn.

JOHN: The name's "John." I'm very pleased.

JOHN hands the urn to NICK.

JOHN: Young man. I have spent most of my life with The Professor looking down at me from that shelf. Trust me. Give The Professor a chance, and he will be more than a burden.

JULIA: John—Nick and I will look after The Professor, just as you have done.

[Scene 3]

JULIA and NICK, in a dreamy mood, are strolling through the cemetery back to campus. NICK holds the urn. At some distance, an elderly man wearing a black sport coat, tie, and hat watches them approach.

HORACE: Hello, Julia. Hello, Nick.

JULIA: Hello. *(With a knowing smile.)* It's very good to meet you.

NICK: Hello . . . Sir . . . You addressed us by name. Do we know you?

HORACE: Well, yes. In a manner of speaking. Also, you are holding my ashes. My name is Horace Smith. I was a professor in the English Department for many years. That was a long time ago. I taught Shakespeare to thousands of young men and women. Also John Milton. I was respected too. Students heeded my words carefully. *(Pause.)* Back in my day, we didn't just do "literary analysis." We used great literature to help students think and feel with greater depth, expand their humanity. Julia, you showed depth of understanding in the crematorium. Nick, you are a little behind Julia in that regard. You will need to learn from her—and from me. I will bring something to your marriage, to your lives. Perhaps to your children. I can still enlarge the human spirit.

JULIA: Thank you, Professor.

HORACE: Julia. Nick. I'm very pleased that my ashes have been entrusted to you. I've been on that crematorium shelf for 59 years. I did everything I could for John—kept him from getting too lonely, lifted his spirits, gave him a broader outlook on life. He didn't have much of an upbringing, and he didn't have a reflective mind until he began taking long, slow gazes at me. I started him reading and thinking, which is the job of a professor. Living with a young couple like you, there will be new shelves for me to watch from and more that I can do. There will be moments when there is something I'll want you to know, to understand. Will you heed me?

JULIA AND NICK: Yes.

HORACE: Very good. Today feels like the first day of a new semester.

The End

Postscript to "Echoes of the Professor"

This play is based on an actual walk that Jean Farkas and I took in the spring of 1968, a few weeks before we graduated from the University of Rochester. We strolled through the large, old Mount Hope Cemetery and came out near a cottage with gingerbread-style ornamentation and a large, totally incongruous industrial smokestack.

We entered and met the crematorium employee, who was happy to have visitors to talk with. This fellow was much less thoughtful than the character "John." He did not in any way venerate the forgotten man he knew only as The Professor. He was simply interested in clearing the dusty old urn off his shelf. However, out of respect for the dead, he was reluctant to throw the urn into the trash, and so he concocted his flimsy rationale: Since college students "have" professors, we should have this one. Although I eagerly accepted the offer of the urn, Jean gave me a fierce look, and so—very reluctantly—I declined. Had we taken The Professor, he would still be with us today. In a sense, he *is* with us today. Although nameless, he is not a forgotten man.

The imaginative conceit underlying this play is that The Professor, although deceased, has a humanizing effect on those around him. He enhanced the life of John, then Nick and Julia, and then the attorney. We know that he will also enhance the lives of Sandra and Sam. He's an impressive man. Perhaps he will have just a bit of an impact on you.

I Have the Time

A 10-minute play by

David K. Farkas

Characters:

Conference Chair: A middle-aged man.

Della Whittaker: A vivacious middle-aged woman.

Della's Friend: A woman in her 30s.

Tom Lockwood: First an assistant professor in his 30s. Then an associate professor about 50 years old.

Nadine: (Offstage voice.) A woman in her 30s.

Lila: A sex worker.

Todd: A bartender.

Anne: A staff member at the Association of Technical Writers.

Lockwood's Daughter: (Offstage voice.) A young woman.

April: An undergraduate student.

Suggested minimum casting:

Tom Lockwood

Conference Chair/Todd

Della Whittaker/Anne

Della's Friend/Nadine/Lila/Lockwood's daughter/April

[Scene 1]

> The CONFERENCE CHAIR has just stepped up to the podium at the luncheon banquet of the annual conference of the Association of Technical Writers. DELLA WHITTAKER is standing nearby, ready to step up to the podium. Facing the podium are five or six chairs. On

two of these chairs DELLA's FRIEND and ASSISTANT PROFESSOR TOM LOCKWOOD happen to be seated next to each other. The rest of the conference audience is understood to be present. There is loud applause suggesting a speaker who is being welcomed.

CONFERENCE CHAIR: Well, folks, aren't we having a great conference!

Gestures for more applause, which he receives.

CONFERENCE CHAIR: The St. Louis Chapter should be very proud. They worked hard to host the 53rd ATW Conference, and all that work surely paid off. I know we're all eager for the next sessions, but we have one more item on our luncheon agenda. Della Whittaker is going to give us a preview of next year's conference, in . . . Pittsburgh! Many of you know Della. She's a Past President of ATW, she's the current President of the Pittsburgh Chapter, and she heads up ATW's National Scholarship Program. There are more than a few young technical writers attending *this conference* who benefitted greatly from an ATW scholarship. Let's welcome Della to the podium.

Gestures for applause, which he receives. DELLA enters and mounts the podium. DELLA and the CONFERENCE CHAIR hug slightly, the CONFERENCE CHAIR exits, and DELLA, brimming with enthusiasm, faces the audience to begin speaking.

DELLA: We have a truly outstanding conference in store for you in Pittsburgh, next September 4th through 7th. The weather should be good, and we will be right downtown at the Radisson. You may not know this, but Downtown Pittsburgh has become an exciting place with innovative restaurants and great shopping. I can't announce the keynote speaker yet, but we're talking to a true luminary in the field of technical writing, someone who will be of great interest to both industry folks and academics. Of course, we have really fun social events planned for each evening, including a Pirates night game against the San Francisco Giants.

DELLA'S voice fades, and she continues in pantomime. LOCKWOOD notices that DELLA'S FRIEND wears a look of agony, and she is struggling not to cry openly.

LOCKWOOD: Are you OK? Are you ill?

DELLA'S FRIEND: I'm not ill. Please, just hold my hand.

She turns toward LOCKWOOD and places both of her hands in his.

DELLA'S FRIEND: Della's dying of cancer. She knows she'll never see next year's conference. I'm sorry. I just needed to tell someone.

LOCKWOOD: Oh, God. Yes, I understand.

DELLA: *(At full volume.)* So, see you all in Pittsburgh!

There is applause. DELLA'S FRIEND and LOCKWOOD applaud mechanically, but he is looking intently into the eyes of DELLA'S FRIEND as she tries to keep her composure. Then, as the applause subsides, they stand and move into the aisle to leave the hall.

DELLA'S FRIEND: How can she do that? How can anyone be that strong?

LOCKWOOD: I don't know. I am so sad. I don't know what else to say.

DELLA'S FRIEND and LOCKWOOD begin to part ways with a final, meaningful glance.

LOCKWOOD: I am so sorry. This is such a tragedy.

DELLA sees LOCKWOOD and calls to him.

DELLA: Professor Lockwood. Tom.

LOCKWOOD: *(Stammering. Almost crying.)* Hello, Della . . . You gave a great conference preview.

DELLA: Thank you . . . Tom, I need to talk to you about something. You've done a great job with the Scholarship Program for the Twin Cities chapter. Everyone recognizes that. I'm asking you to take over for me at the national level. It's just a 3-year commitment, not that much work.

LOCKWOOD: Della, I'm sorry, but that's really not possible. I am already . . .

DELLA: Tom, I know how much you do, and I hate to ask. But, Tom, I need to replace myself in some of my ATW roles. I have really pressing reasons. Please. I have to keep going with next year's conference, but I need to get certain parts of my life in order.

LOCKWOOD is visibly appalled by this request.

LOCKWOOD: Um . . . I don't . . . I . . . I really can't. I just can't.

DELLA: Tom, I need this. I really do. Please, Tom.

LOCKWOOD: OK . . . OK. I'll do it.

DELLA: Thank you so much. I'm breathing easier now. I'll send you some materials, and we can talk on the phone. I'll walk you through everything.

LOCKWOOD: *(Deeply reluctant and unhappy.)* OK, Della.

DELLA: Thanks, Tom. Catch you later.

LOCKWOOD: Goodbye, Della.

They exit.

[Scene 2]

LOCKWOOD is lounging, a bit disheveled, in a chair in his hotel room. He is talking on the phone with his wife, NADINE, who is very angry.

NADINE: What! We talked about this before you left. You promised. No more extra work. No new commitments. Tom, all you care about is your career. One more item on your vita. I don't count. The kids don't count. Your life at home doesn't count. Just your job, just your career. I've had it with you, Tom. I've had it! Take ten more jobs at the conference. I'll make sure you have lots of time for everything.

LOCKWOOD: Nadine. Please, you don't understand. This had nothing to do with my career. It was something else entirely. Please, just let me explain.

NADINE: Don't tell me anything! All I know is that you promised me that your family would start getting a little more of your attention.

LOCKWOOD: Please, Nadine. Just listen to me.

NADINE: There's nothing I want to hear from you. Good . . . bye!

NADINE hangs up. LOCKWOOD is overwhelmed with emotion.

[Scene 3]

LOCKWOOD sits at a small table in the hotel bar. There are two empty drinks and a fresh one on the table. LILA approaches TOM.

LILA: Hi, honey. You must be the most unhappy man in this entire hotel. Are you with the conference?

LOCKWOOD: *(Not quite looking up.)* Yes.

LILA: I'm sorry the conference is going so badly for you.

LOCKWOOD: *(Looking more closely at her.)* It's not the conference. It's trouble at home. My wife.

LILA: Oh, that kind of trouble. I'm really good with that kind of trouble. My name is Lila.

She sits down next to him.

LILA: Believe me, I am really good.

[Scene 4]

Fifteen years later, PROFESSOR LOCKWOOD, tired and morose, is finishing off his second drink at a bar in Minneapolis. LOCKWOOD'S briefcase is on the floor by his bar stool. Even the briefcase looks old and tired.

BARTENDER: Hey, Professor, you want another one?

LOCKWOOD: Yeah, Todd. I'll have one more.

LOCKWOOD'S cell phone rings. He answers it. TODD brings LOCKWOOD his cocktail and exits.

LOCKWOOD: Hello.

ANNE can be seen at the periphery of the stage talking on the phone. LOCKWOOD is sipping his cocktail during the phone call.

ANNE: Hello, Tom. This is Anne Grayson, from the ATW National Office in DC. Is this a good time to talk?

LOCKWOOD: Sure, Anne. It's OK.

ANNE: I'm calling to check in with you regarding the Scholarship Committee. Everyone here at the National Office is so grateful that you've served as Scholarship Chair all these years. You've truly done an outstanding job. I'm calling to confirm that I can set you down for another three-year term.

LOCKWOOD: Yes, Anne. You can.

ANNE: That's great Tom. I am so pleased. One more thing. The Leadership has a new initiative. We want to expand the scholarship program to the international level. For example, India. That's a huge growth area for us. There are a lot of high-tech companies in India, and other countries, ready to support a technical writing scholarship program in their country. We know you can make this a success, but it will entail extra work, so I wanted you to know about the new initiative before you commit to another term.

LOCKWOOD: Yes, it's OK, Anne. I have the time.

ANNE: I am so pleased. Thank you, Professor Lockwood! You contribute so much to ATW.

LOCKWOOD: OK, Anne. Send me whatever materials you have. Goodbye.

> LOCKWOOD ends the call. Then he checks his phone messages, finds one, and plays it. The voice of LOCKWOOD's DAUGHTER is heard from offstage.

LOCKWOOD'S DAUGHTER: Hello, Dad. I just got the birthday present you sent me. The sweater is really nice. Thank you. Sorry, we didn't get to talk. I'll call you on Sunday. Love you, Dad.

> LOCKWOOD puts down the phone.

[Scene 5]

> LOCKWOOD is at his desk in his faculty office, grading a large stack of student papers. There is a knock on the partly open door.

LOCKWOOD: Come in.

> APRIL, one of LOCKWOOD'S students, enters.

LOCKWOOD: Good to see you, April. Take a seat.

APRIL: Professor Lockwood. I've had very good news. I think I've worked out my financial aid for next year. I was really worried about it. But now I'll be able to finish my degree.

LOCKWOOD: That's great, April. I'm so pleased.

APRIL: I just found out that I'm getting a $5000 tuition waiver. And I was chosen for next year's Whittaker Scholarship. That's $4000. That money, along with my student loan, will be enough.

LOCKWOOD: Wonderful! You are an excellent student.

APRIL: *(Hesitantly.)* Professor Lockwood, I know you're very involved with the ATW and their scholarships. Did you help me get the Whittaker scholarship?

LOCKWOOD: No, not at all. I raise money for the scholarship endowment fund. The applications are reviewed by a completely different group of people.

APRIL: Well, however it happened, I'm very grateful to ATW.

LOCKWOOD: You're just the kind of student the Della Whittaker Scholarship is intended for. I know that Della would be pleased that you've been chosen. April . . .

> LOCKWOOD seems to struggle as he speaks.

APRIL: Yes, Professor Lockwood?

LOCKWOOD: April, you're going to get an official notification. Perhaps you already got it. It will say a thing or two about Della Whittaker . . .

> LOCKWOOD begins to get more emotional.

LOCKWOOD: I just . . . I just want to say a few things about Della that they can't put in a notification. She . . . was a very special person. She died relatively young. She died . . .

> LOCKWOOD becomes even more emotional. He begins to lose control.

LOCKWOOD: She was just a . . . very special person. I guess that's all I have to say.

APRIL: Thank you for telling me that, Professor Lockwood. I'll remember what you've said. Professor, are you OK?

LOCKWOOD: Yes. I'm OK. It's just that hearing your news brought back some old memories. That's all.

APRIL: I understand. Were you and Della Whittaker "close"? I mean . . .

LOCKWOOD: No. We weren't really close. We only met a few times. But . . . I guess you could say she had a big impact on my life.

APRIL: Oh. OK. I get it. Are you sure you're OK?

> LOCKWOOD recovers himself.

LOCKWOOD: I'm fine. I just started thinking about some things. Congratulations on the scholarship and the tuition waiver. This is really great news.

APRIL stands and heads toward the door.

APRIL: Thank you, Professor Lockwood. See you in class on Monday.

LOCKWOOD: *(Distantly.)* Yes, April.

LOCKWOOD looks off into space and then out at the audience. He picks up an imaginary student paper from a pile of papers and examines it closely.

LOCKWOOD: Let's see now, "Tom" . . . "Lockwood." Tom, you never seem to graduate. Here you are, one damn semester after another. And I can't say your grades are anything to be proud of. Let's take a look.

Lifts his head to review some kind of imaginary transcript or report card.

LOCKWOOD: "Practicum in Life Satisfaction." Tom, you are failing. You are a lonely, unhappy man . . . "Control of Alcoholic Tendencies." Well, that's a solid B. No one in the Department thinks of you as anything more than a fellow with a drinking problem. You've never shown up obviously drunk at a department meeting, and you're always sober in class. No one knows about the bottle in your briefcase . . . "Other Vices." Hmm, not good, Tom. Not good. You do seem to require occasional female companionship. And not the right kind of female companionship. You might have gotten caught by now, except absolutely no one cares where in the city you go at night. And, you're too smart to get yourself arrested. Well, that's worth a half point extra credit . . . "Maintaining Relationships with Children." Well, Tom, you get an A for effort, but we don't actually give a grade for effort. So, let's see. Your daughter talks to you, and your son does not. Averages to a D, Tom. Sorry. Yes, Nadine gets some of the blame for that. Too bad you can't give her a grade or two . . . "Knowing When to Say No." Della, Oh, Della. It wasn't your fault. But look what you did to me! . . . "Teaching Effectiveness." That's the one grade that pulls up your average, Tom. That and the scholarship money you've raised all these years . . . "Future Prospects." Hmm. I don't see much likelihood of improvement. I think it will be pretty much the same, right up to the end. Graded papers stacked half way to the moon. An army of students and a small army of advisees. Nice kid, that April . . . Oh, wait, all is not grim. With just a little luck they'll be a Thomas Lockwood Scholarship at ATW after you die. "Hello Della Whittaker Scholarship. I'm the new Thomas Lockwood Scholarship. Pleased to meet you. You must remember Della. She was quite a woman, wasn't she!"

The End

Postscript to "I Have the Time"

Tom Lockwood's life is blighted by an imprudent act of kindness. But who could have refused Della Whittaker's request at that moment? I don't believe I could have. Lockwood makes his life worse by relying on sex workers and alcohol, but Nadine's refusal to listen is the beginning of Lockwood's downhill slide.

In the long final monologue, Lockwood assesses his life as though he is grading a student paper. We believe him when he says he can give himself a good grade for teaching. Because he never lost his commitment to teaching and his concern for his students, Lockwood retains some piece of his self-respect.

The opening scene of this play closely follows actual events. My encounter with Della Whittaker's friend was heartbreaking. Then, listening to Della complete her exuberant invitation to attend next year's conference, I was overcome by her display of discipline and her courageous bravado. She was looking at Death and staring it down. When Della completed her speech, Della's friend quickly slipped out of the auditorium. I exchanged a few words with Della, but she did not ask me to take over any committee assignment.

The rest of the play is entirely fiction—except that the play touches my personal life in the final scene when Lockwood breaks down into stammering and tears after April tells him she's received the Della Whittaker Scholarship. During my long career teaching technical communication, several of my students received the Society for

Technical Communication's Della Whittaker Scholarship (which has now been discontinued). When the student told me the good news, I felt the need to say a little about the extraordinary women for whom the scholarship was named. I am not much given to weeping, and I always strived to maintain a professional demeanor with my students— especially undergraduates. But on one occasion I broke into stammering and tears trying to describe the circumstances of Della's speech at that conference.

Graduation

A 10-minute play by

David K. Farkas

Characters:

Jenn: A doctoral student.

Betty: Another doctoral student.

Christine: A former doctoral student, now a cocktail waitress; Also plays the woman at the gallery opening.

Professor Peter Smith: A young professor in their department.

Setting:

Scenes 1, 2, 4, and 5 utilize a split set. On one side of the stage we see a coffee shop table and three chairs. On the other side we see Peter's campus office. Scene 3 takes place downstage of the split set. Scene 6 also takes place downstage of the split set but a few items are brought in to suggest the opening of an exhibit at an art gallery.

[Scene 1]

   A coffee shop with JENN, BETTY, and CHRISTINE sitting together.

JENN: Have you heard anything about Peter? Is he doing any better?

BETTY: I know he was at the last department meeting. So, he must be better, a lot better. But people are saying that he told the chair he wants to take a leave of absence.

JENN: I really need to finish my dissertation. There's no one else in the Department who can do human-robot interaction.

CHRISTINE: He'd probably work with you even if he went on leave.

JENN: I guess. He's that kind of person. But it depends on where he is and how he's feeling. And things would be difficult if his lab shut down. I have no idea what the funding situation is. I can't imagine who would take over.

BETTY: I want to work with him too. I was going to ask him to help me plan out a dissertation topic.

CHRISTINE: The pitfalls of academia. Life is simpler when you're a cocktail waitress. Trust me. I was never cut out to be a professor.

BETTY: The academic world wasn't ready for you either, Christine. Best you stay clear of each other.

JENN: He's lonely. No one has ever seen him with a woman. Or a man either. Reynoldsburg is not a place for a single guy. All the faculty seem to have families. Everything is about families and kids—picnics, Little League. He just works. He's always in the building on weekends.

BETTY: We don't know for sure that he's lonely or what his problem is.

CHRISTINE: Well, I'll bet on the "lonely guy" hypothesis. And I believe there is a solution to his problem—and yours.

JENN and BETTY look at each other wondering what CHRISTINE has in mind.

[Scene 2]

PETER is seated at his office desk. Near the desk is a chair for visitors. JENN is standing at an imagined open doorway. She knocks on the door post.

PETER: Come in.

JENN enters.

JENN: Hello, Professor Smith . . . Peter. How are you?

Without any hesitation, she sits in the office chair.

JENN: I'm not here to talk about my research. I just wanted to find out whether you're feeling OK.

PETER: Thanks. I'm OK, Jenn. I think I'll be ready when the new quarter begins. I've had a rough time of it. No secret about that. I feel terrible about not finishing my classes last quarter. All those students without final grades. And, I haven't been much help to you and the other doctoral students.

JENN: We're doin' OK, for now at least . . . Peter, there are rumors you might be leaving.

PETER: I need to be open with everyone. I'm not sure I'll continue next year. I've asked for a medical leave. I don't know what I'll do. I'm from Minneapolis, and I have family there. I think I'll go back, at least for a while. Fortunately, money is not a pressing concern for me. I can take my time deciding what to do next. If I leave, I'm probably burning my bridges as far as academia is concerned. I'd feel obligated to reveal my breakdown, and any department that looked at me would probably find out anyway. I can certainly find an interesting industry job or just consult part-time.

JENN: Betty and I were talking. Other folks too. We value you so much—as a professor, as a person, as a friend. I hope you appreciate just how much your students like and respect you.

PETER: That's great to hear. Really it is.

JENN: Christine too. We think that—maybe—you are lonely. Living alone and . . . lonely. Reynoldsburg is no town for a single man. Everything is geared for families, and it's no place for a man—unless you're an undergraduate—to meet a woman.

PETER: That might describe my situation.

JENN: Peter, are you gay? It's a rude question, an inappropriate question, but I need to know. There's nothing wrong with being gay. That's a given. But, still, I'm asking.

PETER: I'm not gay. I am a healthy, heterosexual man. I know why you asked. I'm "shy." Not gay, just shy. I was shy in high school, in college, and now. I've had relationships, but they started in unusual ways—ways that you just can't make happen when you want to.

JENN: Life is full of surprises. You just never know what lies ahead. Maybe your life will change . . . in terms of relationships.

PETER: Maybe so. I appreciate the visit, Jenn. If I leave Reynoldsburg, you're one of the people I will miss most.

[Scene 3]

> JENN, BETTY, and CHRISTINE are standing downstage. CHRISTINE is standing behind a photographer's tripod that holds a smartphone.

JENN: OK, who's first?

CHRISTINE: One of you goes first. I'm perfectly willing to take off my clothes—for men, for women, for the camera, in the check-out line at a supermarket. But you two are the beneficiaries of this plan. I'm just in it to help my dear friends finish up their doctorates.

BETTY: And because you've been half-crazy your whole life.

CHRISTINE: Maybe so. But I'm the photographer, so one of you will be first, the other will be second, and I'll be third. When it's my turn, I'll plan the shot and set the timer. I'm directing this photoshoot, so I give the orders . . . Jenn, you're first. Take it off, everything. Then look at me. I want you sexy, but not vulgar. *(Now in a comically refined accent.)* Professor Smith is a very refined, genteel fellow.

BETTY: That's right. Not vulgar. Doctoral-student sexy.

> JENN shyly does a model's turn, does another one less shyly, strikes a sexy pose or two, and begins to undress.

[Scene 4]

> PETER is at his office desk. The door is open. Jenn knocks on the door post.

PETER: Come in.

JENN: Hello, Peter. How are you?

PETER: I'm OK. A little better.

> She takes a seat.

PETER: Jenn, I think you said something about a book you wanted me to see.

JENN: Yes, I have it right here. It's not exactly a book. It's a . . . photo album. It hasn't been published. It won't be published. In fact, this is the only copy, and it may be burned and in the trash by the end of the day.

PETER: I'm truly puzzled.

JENN: *(Pulling up her chair closer to PETER'S.)* Let me show you, Peter. Hold on to your seat.

She opens the album.

PETER: What? What is this?

JENN: *(Mischievously.)* You know what this is, Peter. It's me. *(Turning the page.)* And this is also me.

PETER: Why are you doing this? What's going on?

JENN: And this is Betty. Here's another shot of Betty. She looks great, doesn't she? And here's Christine, the star of the show. We took these a week ago. We took them just for you. Christine says "hello." She says you were one of her favorite professors.

PETER: Jenn, I think you should take your book and leave my office.

JENN: Here's the deal, short and sweet. You stay at Tech for at least two more academic years—we hope it's forever. Betty and I will both complete degrees working in your lab, with you as dissertation director. During this time, we guarantee you female "companionship"—three attractive young women. Christine is in it just for fun. You know Christine.

PETER: "A"—this is crazy. "B"—this is unethical. "C"—I'd get fired for having sexual relations with students. "D". . .

As PETER hesitates, JENN interrupts.

JENN: "C" is true enough. But we will be very, very discrete. We all know how high the stakes are. Unethical? I'm not so sure. Usually, it's the male professor who exercises power over his female students. But this is something different. For the record, we're the "aggressors." All we want is for you to keep your job and fulfill your regular duties. We get no special treatment. What's wrong with that? *(Extends the book.)* Take another look, Peter. Christine is a good photographer, isn't she? Don't be shy. It's natural for a man to want to look. Peter, we are really very fond of you.

PETER: Let's get back to "A," "crazy." This seems like a Christine idea. Tell me if I'm right.

JENN: Well, yes.

PETER: I appreciate your good intentions, but this is not well thought out. I don't like what this idea implies about men and, in particular, about me. You three provide sex and my problems are solved?

JENN: OK, I understand. I'm sorry. Christine has a strong personality. It seemed like the right thing—for us and for you.

PETER: I do appreciate the good intentions. And that little photo album is . . . something else!

JENN: What if we go slow, Betty and me. We'll leave Christine out of it. This will be a special relationship—based on the genuine affection we feel. We'll let it go where it goes. Maybe into sex. Maybe just friendship. Maybe stop it altogether if it's not working out. Time will tell. Can you respect this kind of arrangement? Will you go forward with it?

PETER: It's something I'd need to think about. It's something you and Betty need to think about as well.

[Scene 5]

> JENN, BETTY, and CHRISTINE are sitting together at the coffee shop. Almost two years have gone by.

JENN: I've got the date set for my final defense.

BETTY: Good for you. I'm not too far behind. I have all my data analyzed and written up. I'm just doing a revision on the final chapter. When do you go to Purdue?

JENN: Next week. They seem really interested.

BETTY: It's been an unusual two years. When we began our "special relationship" with Peter, he was definitely closer to you. But somehow it all moved in my direction. Sometimes I imagine that we're married, or that we could be headed that way. But that's not in the cards. We are not quite lifetime companions. Besides, his career is here, and I have to start my own career somewhere else—with my own lab.

JENN: Betty, we need to figure out the end game. I'm sure Peter is wondering what the next phase of his life is going to be. When the time comes and he has to face up to your leaving, do you think he'll find another woman? Do you think you . . . we . . . could arrange a date for him?

44

BETTY: I have my doubts. He will surely want another relationship, but I doubt he's prepared to find himself a woman.

CHRISTINE: I think maybe I have an answer. When it comes to relationships, Peter is like an animal that's been raised in captivity. Never had to hunt for his dinner. So . . . we teach him to hunt, so we can let him out in the wild!

JENN: What?

BETTY: Christine may in fact have a workable idea.

CHRISTINE: You bet I have. We can teach him—the three of us. "Peter, first you scan the room. You're looking for a woman who . . . Then, you walk up to her. You say . . ." We can do it step by step . . . just up to the very end. That part he knows. We can have If/Then scenarios: "If the woman says X, you say Y. If she does this, you do that." Make it like a course.

JENN: Would he do it?

BETTY: I think he might. Peter's been taking courses, designing courses, and teaching courses since he was 18. If we present this as one more "advanced degree" he needs to earn, he'll likely give it a shot. He does trust me. He trusts *us.*

JENN: But would he succeed? Would he get past his shyness? What if he "went out on the hunt" and failed miserably? Then he'd be worse off than ever.

CHRISTINE: We could have a setup, a ringer. He thinks he's picking up a woman, but she's just waiting for him, all set up in advance. Lots of my friends would do it.

BETTY: No. Or, only as a last resort.

[Scene 6]

An art gallery opening, which is indicated by several real or imagined photographs hanging on a real or imagined wall and by a folding cocktail table with a white tablecloth and glasses of champagne. JENN and BETTY are standing close together at the periphery. PETER approaches a woman looking at a photograph.

PETER: I really like the color palette. What do you think?

WOMAN: Judging by your tie and jacket, you have no business commenting on color palettes!

> She walks away briskly and exits. PETER glances unhappily at JENN and BETTY. They smile back encouragingly.

BETTY: What a bitch that woman is. The tie goes just fine with his jacket.

JENN: Well, he took the plunge.

BETTY: Yes, what he did was good. It just didn't work out.

JENN: I have high hopes. He was very "coachable," and he's definitely more confident.

> PETER walks downstage left or right and approaches an unseen person who is offstage. JENN and BETTY follow him with their gaze.

BETTY: He's looking at another woman. The one in the yellow dress.

JENN: There he goes.

PETER: *(To unseen woman.)* We can certainly see a major shift in Doisneau's aesthetic after the war years. Don't you think so?

JENN: They are talking. Mr. Smooth! Go Peter.

> After a few moments, PETER, speaking in pantomime, escorts the unseen woman upstage and exits.

BETTY: I think the three of us are on track for graduation.

The End

Postscript to "Graduation"

"Graduation" is a sex-themed play that caused me a lot of trouble. I write my 10-minute plays primarily for the very informal Goat Hill Theater that Jean Farkas and I have organized in our small suburb of Lake Forest Park, just north of Seattle. A group of us get together periodically and perform a program of three or four 10-minute plays for ourselves and some friends. We perform in a living room, a backyard, or a venue such as the community room of a local library. For more information about doing your own homebrew theater, see David K. Farkas, *Performing 10-Minute Plays with Friends,* Amazon/Kindle, 2023.

When we performed "Graduation," everyone was fully engaged, but engaged doesn't necessarily mean pleased. We always conduct a talk-back after the plays are performed, and "Graduation" generated a lot of disapproval. About half of our group declared the play degrading to women. Jean Farkas hated the play when she first read the script and advised me not to stage it. Although I've made significant revisions for this collection, she still doesn't like it.

Not everyone disapproved, however. One member of the audience, a female academic, liked the play and had no objection to the actions of the women. "To get my dissertation finished, I'd have jumped into bed with my dissertation director in an instant." I wondered what her husband thought about this. I'll mention here that a later play in this collection, "The Day of the Deal," depicts a situation in which a woman agrees to sex with a stranger in order to get her dissertation published.

I staunchly denied that the play degraded women: These women are not victims who have been coerced into sex. Nor are they connivers who trade sex for special treatment. They genuinely like Peter and want to lift him from his loneliness and depression. So is it wrong to devise a plan that both helps Peter and enables Jenn and Betty to complete their doctoral research under his direction?

After our performance, a well-regarded female playwright read the script and offered a perceptive response. The problem with the play, she said, is that it degrades *men*. It implies that if a man is getting laid, he's happy. With this feedback in mind, I made some revisions, First, I had Peter voice this idea. Second, I put more emphasis on companionship and less on sex. Finally, in the revised version, Christine—the most sexually focused of the women—is no longer one of Peter's lovers.

I faced one more dilemma revising the play. There is nothing wrong, I think, with having Jenn, Betty, and Christine tutor Peter in the social skills he will need to meet women on his own. But the use of hunting as a metaphor for obtaining a romantic partner can be questioned:

CHRISTINE: When it comes to relationships, Peter is like an animal that's been raised in captivity. Never had to hunt for his dinner. So . . . we teach him to hunt, so we can let him out in the wild!

Despite some unease, I kept this speech.

The origin of the play was my recollection of a remark made long ago by my brother, who was an assistant professor of psychology at a prestigious but rural university. He complained that it was not easy for him to find female companionship. He wasn't going to date students, and in this family-oriented little town there were not many appropriate women. I let my imagination loose on this remark and came up with this play.

Quality Work

A 10-minute play by

David K. Farkas

Setting:

Various locations on the campus of a large university, especially the office of Eric Sloane's department chair.

Characters:

Eric Sloane: Recently hired as an associate professor. His cheerful demeanor and non-committal responses to Arlene's questions mask his stubborn resistance to her wishes.

Arlene (Last name never used): Hard-working department chair.

Server at Reception

Female Student 1

Female Student 2

Male Student 1

Male Student 2

Singer

Suggested minimum casting:

Eric Sloane

Arlene

Male Student 1/Male Student 2/possibly the Singer/possibly the Server at the reception

Female Student 1/Female Student 2/possibly the Singer/possibly the Server at the reception

[Scene 1]

> ERIC walks through the open door of ARLENE'S office. She steps from behind her desk, takes a seat on a comfortable chair by a small coffee table and beckons for ERIC to take a similar seat.

ARLENE: Eric, thanks for stopping by.

ERIC: Sure.

ARLENE: Looks like you're pretty well settled in the department. Last quarter certainly seems to have gone well for you.

ERIC: Yes, I think so.

ARLENE: That's great. But there *is* something I would like to ask you about.

ERIC: Sure.

ARLENE: You seem to have given *a lot* of "incomplete" grades last quarter. About 20% of the students in your undergraduate course received I's. And over a third of your graduate students received I's. That's a lot of incomplete grades.

> ERIC nods noncommittally.

ARLENE: Actually, that's about as many as the rest of the department put together.

ERIC: If you say so.

ARLENE: Perhaps, your assignments are too complicated. This is a public university, nothing like Wesleyan. Almost all of our students have jobs—half-time or even more. They have less time to work on their term papers than what you're used to.

ERIC: Perhaps. But I think my assignments are about the same as the rest of the faculty.

ARLENE: How many pages do you ask for?

ERIC: I treat length as kind of a general guideline, but I expect about 12 pages for undergraduates and about 20 for grad students.

ARLENE: Yes. That's about standard.

ERIC: But there is one thing . . . I don't have due dates.

ARLENE: What!?

ERIC: I tell the students that I'd like to get their papers on such and such a date, but I make it clear that the deadline is not mandatory. They can take longer if they want to.

ARLENE: How much longer?

ERIC: As long as they'd like. I tell them, "When it's done, I'll grade it."

ARLENE: So the papers just dribble in?

ERIC: Not exactly. I get quite a few papers on the due date.

ARLENE: "Quite a few by the due date"! Most faculty get *all* their papers on the due date, with maybe one or two exceptions. And a student whose paper is late gets an extension—maybe one more week or something like that. No instructor says "I'll wait forever."

ERIC: That's what I do.

ARLENE: This must be very inconvenient for you. I like to get the full batch of papers, spend a few days grading them, and then I'm done with that assignment.

ERIC: Yes, it is inconvenient. When a paper comes in really late, like months late or years late, it may take me a while to remember what the assignment was all about.

ARLENE: So, why do you do it?

ERIC: That's how Gordon O'Brien, my dissertation director, did it. Undergraduate courses, graduate courses, thesis chapters. He said, "I don't want to grade rushed work. I don't want to grade fatigue. I want to read the best work you can do. Nothing else."

ARLENE: I assume he had a lot of incompletes.

ERIC: Yes, just about every grad student owed him something. There was one paper where I just kept working and working. I think I gave it to him a year late.

ARLENE: A good paper, I assume.

ERIC: Very good. That's what Gordon wanted.

ARLENE: I see. I don't recall this coming up during your job interview.

ERIC: No, I don't think it did.

[Scene 2]

> ERIC and ARLENE stand together with glasses of wine. They are standing downstage from the set that represents ARLENE's office. They are a little more formally dressed. A SERVER comes with a platter of appetizers. They each take one from the tray.

ERIC: Nice reception.

ARLENE: That's what we get when they're hosted by the dean's office . . . Eric, I took a look at your teaching evaluations from last quarter. The numerical scores were high—that's great. Normally when numerical scores are high, I don't bother reading the comments. A lot of them are scribbled, barely legible. But in this case, because there were so many incomplete grades, I did read the comments.

ERIC: OK.

ARLENE: Eric, when we talked in my office, you told me that you didn't set due dates. You didn't tell me that you won't *take* the papers when students try to submit them. That's what some of the students seemed to be saying in their comments.

ERIC: That's not quite accurate. I'll take any paper. I just say to the class, "If this is your best work, I'll take your paper. If not, please don't submit it." Some students think about what they wrote and change their mind about submitting the paper. Or, a student will hand me a paper in the hallway and say, "Sorry, but it didn't really come out great. I was in a rush." So, I say, "I don't want to grade rushed work. I'll take it some other time."

ARLENE: You're basically guilt-tripping your students.

ERIC: If you mean that asking students for their best work is a "guilt trip," then yes.

> There is the sound of a spoon clanking against a glass. ARLENE and ERIC turn their heads toward the sound.

ARLENE: Looks like the Dean is going to speak. We'll have to continue this discussion later.

ERIC: Sure.

ARLENE: *(Aside to audience.)* Goddamn! If I were working in any other place than a university, I could just *tell* Eric what I want him to do.

[Scene 3]

ERIC and ARLENE are standing in a hallway of a classroom building. ERIC is carrying books and papers. He has apparently just left class.

ARLENE: Eric, let's chat for a moment, shall we?

ERIC: Sure.

ERIC and ARLENE suddenly turn their heads as though someone or something just came down the hallway at a high rate of speed.

ARLENE: What was that?

ERIC: I think it may have been Karl. He owes me three incompletes, and he tends to just speed by me in the building.

ARLENE: Oh.

ERIC and ARLENE turn their heads again, this time in a different direction.

ARLENE: What was *that?*

ERIC: I think it might have been Jenny Simpson darting into the ladies' room to avoid me. She does that.

ARLENE: She owes you an incomplete or two?

ERIC: Yep.

FEMALE STUDENT 1 approaches and speaks in a rushed voice as she speeds down the hallway without slowing down.

FEMALE STUDENT 1: Hello, Professor.

MALE STUDENT 1 enters and approaches ERIC with trepidation.

MALE STUDENT 1: Dr. Sloane, you'll have my thesis chapter soon. Real soon. Maybe three more months.

ERIC begins to respond, but the student disappears.

ARLENE: Eric, do you see a problem here?

FEMALE STUDENT 2 and MALE STUDENT 2 enter in a relaxed manner. Then they spot ERIC and stop dead in their tracks.

FEMALE STUDENT 2: There's Sloane!

They turn back and exit running in the direction from which they came.

ARLENE: I certainly don't want to impinge on your academic freedom. But—and try to be reasonable, Eric. *(Irritation enters her voice.)* Do . . . you . . . see . . . a . . . problem . . . here?

ERIC: Hmmm. Perhaps there's something to what you're saying.

ERIC and ARLENE exit.

There is a musical interlude in which two students enter and sing a few lines to a tune borrowed from the Stephen Foster song, "I Dream of Jeanie with the Light Brown Hair."

SINGERS:

I dream of freedom from these grades of "Incomplete,"

Inflicted upon me by Professor Eric Sloane.

I dream of freedom from these grades of "Incomplete,"

Inflicted upon me by Professor Eric Sloane.

SINGERS exit.

[Scene 4]

ARLENE and ERIC enter from the opposite direction. ERIC is carrying different books and papers or perhaps an old briefcase. They are both dressed somewhat differently. As they meet at center stage, ARLENE stops to speak with ERIC. She does not bother with a greeting and small talk.

ARLENE: Eric, I assume you saw yesterday's email from the registrar's office.

ERIC: I did.

ARLENE: You understand the implications? I mean in regard to your practice of giving out so many incomplete grades.

ERIC: I believe I do.

ARLENE: Just to spell it out for you. Starting next quarter, an "I" grade doesn't disappear when the student finishes the course. It stays on the student's transcript *forever* alongside the student's final grade. It shows potential employers, graduate school admissions committees—everyone—that the student didn't complete the course on time. I think you're going to have to stop giving out so many incomplete grades. Don't you agree, Eric?

ERIC: I believe you're right about that.

 ARLENE smiles with cautious satisfaction.

ARLENE: OK then!

 ERIC nods non-committedly and exits. ARLENE speaks to herself and to the audience.

ARLENE: I guess that's one headache taken care of. This is looking like a good day.

[Scene 5]

 ARLENE and ERIC are seated, frozen, by the coffee table in her office. ARLENE does not look happy. The SINGER enters and sings a few lines to a tune borrowed from "I Dream of Jeanie with the Light Brown Hair." ARLENE hums to the singing. Then the SINGER exits.

SINGER (with ARLENE humming)**:**

I dream of colleagues who cooperate,

And make it easier to be department chair.

I dream of colleagues who cooperate,

And make it *(Speaks the next four words.)* —just a little easier—to be department chair.

ARLENE: Eric, are you feeling alright?

ERIC: Sure.

ARLENE: I mean, any illness?

ERIC: No, I'm totally fine.

ARLENE: A big problem at home? Some kind of crisis?

ERIC: No.

ARLENE: Then let me ask you about all these X grades you've given. The grade of X is to be given only under very special circumstances, when the instructor is unable to complete the grading that is necessary to assign the student a grade in the course. That's almost always illness. But you say you haven't been ill and haven't had any special problem.

ERIC: The University has its definition of an X grade—and I have mine.

ARLENE: What do you mean?

ERIC: My X grade is like an incomplete, except when the student completes the course, the X grade disappears from the student's transcript just like the old incompletes used to do.

ARLENE: But, Eric, you are making a false statement to the University, lying, in effect. You're claiming that it's *your* fault that the student couldn't complete the course.

ERIC: If I'm lying, I'm only lying to a computer system.

ARLENE: But consider the disruption this whole crazy business is causing your students. For the whole department. We're getting a whole backlog of students who don't graduate because they owe you work. Every time you walk down the hall, students run from the building. Do you like that?

ERIC: No.

ARLENE: I would never impinge on your academic freedom. And, yes, you were hired with tenure. But we *do* need to fix this.

ERIC: Hmmm. I see your point.

ARLENE: You like perfectionists. I like perfectionists. But you're punishing our most conscientious students. Some kind of compromise is in order.

ERIC: Perhaps so.

ARLENE: My article on *Paradise Lost* might have been a tiny bit better if I'd learned to read 17th century Dutch instead of reading Joost van den Vondel [Yost van den Rohn-del] in translation. Would you say I shouldn't have published the article because it wasn't my absolute best possible work?

ERIC: Umm.

ARLENE: What would your dissertation director say about that?

ERIC: I can't ask him. He died two years ago. He was riding his motorcycle in bad weather.

ARLENE: I'm sorry about that . . . How many incompletes did he leave behind when he died?

ERIC: I wouldn't know . . . Probably a lot.

ARLENE: And who is going to finish up his students? That's a big mess. Your extreme insistence on quality work is full of problems. Can't you recognize that?

ERIC: What if I were to say in class, "I don't want to see your assignment unless you are . . . "proud of your work"?

ARLENE: I can live with that. But how about taking it down just one notch? Some folks have a much higher bar than others for what makes them "proud." How about something just a little less dependent on the student's psychological make-up?

ERIC: OK. OK. I could tell them . . . "I only want to see your work if it's quality work." No rushed work. No fatigue. Quality work."

ARLENE: Yes! Yes! Do we have agreement on this?

ERIC: We do.

ARLENE: And one more thing. I'd like to tell those students who are hiding from you, that you've eased up on this idea of only taking their best work.

ERIC: I don't know. I'd have to think about that.

ARLENE: Eric, aren't you tired of having students hide from you when you walk down the hallway? Don't you feel bad about keeping students from graduating?

ERIC: OK. OK. You can tell my students that I've eased up. They can come out of hiding.

ARLENE: Excellent! Excellent. I'm so glad we had this little talk.

ERIC: Yes.

ARLENE: And you'll stop assigning "X" grades? You will stop violating University grading policy?

ERIC: No, I will not. Those are "Sloane Incomplete" grades.

ARLENE: *(Resignedly.)* OK. OK. I'll forget I ever noticed all your X grades.

>   ERIC nods with satisfaction. ARLENE subtly signals that the meeting is over. ERIC picks up his briefcase and prepares to leave.

ARLENE: Thank you, Eric, for being so cooperative.

ARLENE: *(Aside to audience.)* I can't believe I just said that!

ERIC: Sure, I always aim to be cooperative, collegial—all that good stuff.

>   ERIC exits. ARLENE stands in order to move back to her desk chair and speaks again to the audience.

ARLENE: "Cooperative"! "Collegial"! My God! What a pain in the butt he is! And I have a dozen more faculty problems to deal with. People who can't work together. Salary inequities. More arguments about travel money. At least dealing with Eric wasn't a hit on my budget. It is not easy being chair. Who do I talk to now? To Denise, about the grievance she just filed? To Randall, who comes to class 20 minutes late day after day?

>   ARLENE sings a few lines to a tune borrowed from "I Dream of Jeanie with the Light Brown Hair."

ARLENE:

I dream of colleagues who cooperate,
And do not drive me, half out of my mind.
I dream of colleagues who cooperate,
And do not drive me, half out of my mind.

The End

Postscript to "Quality Work"

Eric Sloane's refusal to specify a due date for assignments may or may not be a good idea. Perhaps it's something that works for him, as it seems to have worked, at least in certain respects, for his mentor. On the other hand, Eric's insistence that his students submit only their "best work" is plainly a bad idea. In effect, he is guilt tripping his students, just as Arlene tells him.

In a corporate setting, she would simply order Eric to follow standard procedures, and he would have to comply. But in a university environment, Eric retains control of his instructional methods, and so Arlene must persuade him. After a while, Eric *is* persuaded, and he eases off on the unrealistic level of quality he asks from his students. Perhaps this revised assignment policy will work. Perhaps other faculty will adopt some or part of Eric's approach. Perhaps the new policy will continue to cause problems, prompting Arlene to cajole Eric once again. But although Eric is stubborn and exasperating in his evasiveness, Eric *does* respond to a compelling argument. He is persuadable.

The play, then, celebrates, in a whimsical manner, faculty autonomy and collegiality rather than administrative control. The special culture of the university makes heavy demands on department chairs, but Arlene, despite some complaining and a bit of self-pity, proves up to the task.

Although Eric retains his autonomy, we see the corporate university closing in on him. The corporate university wants to move the maximum number of students through the system as smoothly as possible, and their new incomplete policy is part of that effort. Eric's X-grade trick won't work forever.

Finally, the play dodges the problem of the faculty member who abuses their academic freedom, who employs dysfunctional and even abusive teaching methods and who is *not* persuadable. I saw some of this during my teaching career, although it was infrequent. While this kind of situation falls outside the scope of this short play, universities must have the authority to intervene when truly necessary.

The next play in this collection offers another look at the same dynamic: the unworthy values and agenda of the central administration vs. the independent behavior of faculty—with Ming, the department chair, caught in the middle. But, like Arlene, Ming's core values are sound, and she finishes up on the right side of things.

Travel Money

A 10-minute play by

David K. Farkas

Characters:

Mary Bartlett: Full professor in an unspecified humanities department of a large university. She is not young, is highly respected, and often chairs committees.

Emma Columbo: Associate professor. She is poised and proper and has a strong sense of fairness and ethics.

Fred Brennan: Assistant professor. Often brash and intemperate.

Sid Warkowski: Assistant professor. Looks out for "Number One."

Ming Dong: Full professor and department chair. Spends most of her time as an administrator. Her name should be changed if a Chinese actor is not cast.

Setting:

A small conference room with nondescript furnishings. Certain items suggest a university conference room. The faculty members have laptops, tablets, and yellow pads—all for taking notes.

[Scene 1]

    SID, FRED, and EMMA are seated at a small conference table.

SID: The Department is getting travel money! Can you believe it?

FRED: Amazing. And it's not coming from the Dean. It's going to be our own money.

    MARY enters quietly and takes a seat at the head of the table.

FRED: One million dollars in memory of Sharon Barker. Do we even know who she is—was?

EMMA: She's the mother of one of Terry Westen's tech buddies. She studied in our department decades ago.

FRED: One million dollars! I guess that's a billionaire's way of saying "Sorry 'bout your mom." Works for me.

MARY: *(Glances at watch.)* OK. Let's get started. It's nice to be chairing a meeting where something good has happened. Not just the usual cutbacks and reductions . . . Someone has to take minutes.

No obvious response from faculty members.

MARY: *(Looks around the table.)* Someone has to take minutes. Sid, I believe it's been a while since you took minutes.

SID: All right.

SID will take the minutes throughout the meeting.

MARY: Thank you, Sid . . . Well, everyone has heard the news. After years and years without travel money, the department now has a professional development endowment, courtesy of Terry Westen. He's given a ton of money to Computer Science and Electrical Engineering. This is his first gift to a humanities department. Might well be his last. He's not a humanities type of guy.

FRED: Definitely not. His level of human development is definitely questioned in some circles. He's one of the "bad boys" of the big-league tech world.

SID: What's his company?

FRED: Avocado AI. That's his main company, anyway. They make super-intelligent holographic avatars. Some high schools now have virtual guidance counselors. Avocado pension fund managers are more successful than human ones. There are a few Avocado AI avatars leading Protestant and Jewish congregations. Very hip. The Roman Catholic Church is saying no.

EMMA: I'm a Lutheran. But before I'd attend that kind of service, I'd find myself an old-fashioned graven image.

MARY: We should get started . . . This is the initial meeting of the committee on travel money. I spoke with Ming this morning. She wants us to give her a set of priorities that will determine how much money each faculty member will receive in any given year. We might also fund travel for Ph.D. candidates, although that can get expensive. Ming remembers that way back, when we got travel money from the Dean, allocating the money was a huge headache. Lots of long meetings, arguments, complaints. Ming wants to avoid all that this time.

EMMA: Won't be easy.

MARY: Hard or easy. That's what she wants us to do . . . The million dollars should throw off about 25K each year. We could just divide that evenly among all the applicants. If we include Ph.D. students in the funding, we'll likely get a total of about 20 applications in a year. That's 1250 dollars for each person. Not enough to cover the cost of most conferences, but a big help. However, splitting the money equally among all the applicants isn't necessarily equitable. As you know, there are all kinds of special circumstances to consider—good reasons why some folks should get more than others.

EMMA: I say that funding—generous funding—for Ph.D. students is essential. They absolutely need publications and conference presentations on their vitas when they go on the job market. They can't possibly pay for that out of their teaching assistant salaries. Some of our Ph.D. students would like to present at two conferences in a year.

FRED: But what if the Ph.D. student is married to a corporate lawyer? Do we take that into consideration?

MARY: Hmm. There's a can of worms. Let's leave it alone for now.

SID: Well, we obviously need to give special consideration to assistant professors. To get tenure and promotion, *we* need to present papers at conferences. Full professors should get the least priority. They don't need to do anything, and they make real money.

MARY: Not that much money, I can assure you. But, yes, I see your point.

EMMA: We need to give some priority to associate professors working toward promotion to full professor. They need to present at conferences too.

SID: What about associate professors who have given up on getting promoted? Those folks are low priority, just like the full professors.

FRED: That sounds like a fun task. Ask all the associate professors if they self-identify as "I've given up all hope of getting promoted."

EMMA: I sort of object to everything we're doing. Well, most everything. We're assuming that the whole purpose of going to a conference is to present a paper. Don't some people go to conferences to *learn* something? Even an associate professor who has "given up on getting promoted" should be able to go to a conference, with travel money, in order to keep up with their field.

MARY: That's a good point. We want everyone to teach well.

FRED: And conferences differ in cost. Some are local. You can just drive to them. Also, hotel rooms in places like New York City are super-expensive. Some conferences run four days, others only three or even two. Some are Zoom conferences—there's just a registration fee.

SID: Two years ago, I went to a conference to receive a research award. If I hadn't shown up, the department would have looked bad. But I wasn't presenting, and the conference was in Boise. You have no idea how expensive it is to fly to Boise. So much for replacing my rotted-out back deck that year.

MARY: OK. OK. We're definitely in the soup. Let's adjourn. I'll ask everyone to write up a "priorities statement." Say how you think we should prioritize the travel money. I'll need your priorities statement in two weeks. Thanksgiving break is coming up, so our next meeting will be in three weeks . . . I can see what Ming was worried about. Looks like figuring out a set of priorities will be a long process. Then, when Ming actually uses it, folks will still be coming back to her with some reason why they should have gotten more money.

SID: But, at least, there's something to give out, rather than deciding what we need to cut.

MARY: True enough. Do I hear a motion to adjourn?

EVERYONE: "Adjourn." "I move to adjourn." "I second."

They exit.

[Scene 2]

> The faculty members drift onto the stage and take their seats for the meeting. MARY is last to arrive.

MARY: OK. Who will take the minutes? Last time it was Sid.

FRED: I'll do it.

> FRED takes minutes throughout the meeting.

MARY: I have big news to report to you. Last week Terry Westen checked in with Ming about his donation. They put me on the call. Ming and I told the truth—that we're having big trouble setting priorities to divide up the travel funds. Westen laughed and said this sounds like an AI problem. That's his thing. So he's ginning up an app just for us. Just a personal project. His idea of fun. He's doing it quick—but of course he's a genius, and anything he does will be amazing. He's calling it "Seymour" because it "Sees" "More" than we do.

FRED: That's like . . . so Terry Westen.

EMMA: Is this something we can really use?

MARY: Westen promises the app will be totally easy to use.

EMMA: I'm suspicious.

SID: But this is Terry Westen honoring his friend's deceased mother. If he's ever going to play it straight, this is the time.

EMMA: I'm still suspicious. What else did he say?

MARY: He's using some software modules from Avocado AI—machine learning, fuzzy logic, natural language understanding—all that stuff. That's why he can do it so fast. But he won't have time to fully test it, so it's ours—as is—you might say. It lives in the cloud, so we don't need to maintain it. We just use it. We enter general statements such as "Assistant Professors need to go to conferences to earn tenure and promotion." We give each statement a priority number between 1 and 10. Seymour generates a priority model based on what we've told it. Then we upload each faculty member's travel money request, and Seymour applies the model. Abracadabra. Each faculty member will receive an email from Seymour stating his or her allocation, along with a brief explanation of how Seymour made the decision.

FRED: Not human, but at least it's transparent.

MARY: Ming, of course, sees everyone's allocation.

EMMA: What if we don't like what Seymour does?

MARY: If Ming overrides one or more of Seymour's decisions, Seymour can recalculate all the allocations. He uses this feedback to improve next year's allocation model. Westen said that if we don't like Seymour, we can just forget about him.

SID: So, let's try it. What have we got to lose?

There are shrugs from the faculty.

MARY: OK. So I tell Ming that we've agreed to employ Seymour to allocate our travel money. Voice vote.

EVERYONE: "Yes." "I second." "Yeah."

[Scene 3]

FRED walks across the stage, holding a tablet and reading an email generated by Seymour. He pauses as he reads.

FRED: *(Reading.)* Fred Brennan, your travel money allocation for this year is $1725. As you specified, the money has been sent to your PayPal account. Your allocation is based on the following considerations: (1) You are an assistant professor working toward tenure and promotion. (2) You are presenting rather than just attending the conference. (3) The conference is relatively expensive: it requires an airline flight, it's a 3-day conference, and hotel rooms are expensive in the conference city.

FRED makes a gesture that indicates that he's pleased. Then, as he reads further, he exhibits great surprise.

FRED: Fred, I fully respect faculty development and the value of conference participation. However, I have concluded that this is not the optimum use of your travel money allocation. Although I cannot provide details, I have identified some very promising investment opportunities. I invite you to tap "Invest."

FRED looks around furtively, taps his tablet, and rushes offstage. Now SID enters and crosses the stage holding a smartphone. He is half-way through reading a similar email message.

SID: Sid Warkowski, your allocation is based on the following considerations. (1) You are an assistant professor. (2) The conference is within easy driving distance. (3) Because you are an invited speaker, your registration fee has been waived. Sid, I fully respect faculty development and the value of conference participation. However, . . .

> SID now reads silently. He is at a fever pitch of excitement. SID exits. EMMA enters holding a laptop awkwardly and reading silently.

EMMA: Holy shit! Totally outrageous! Seymour is inviting us to violate University regulations, maybe state law. *(Contemptuously.)* That's what happens when you let an emotionally underdeveloped software guru take over human decision-making.

> EMMA exits still reading but shaking her head in disapproval.

[Scene 4]

> EMMA, SID, DAVID, and MARY are seated at the conference table. MING has joined them and sits at the head of the table. She is angry.

MING: I am appalled. Six members of this department authorized Seymour to convert their travel money allocation into a personal investment. That money was not a direct gift to you from Westen. It was University money. What you did is tantamount to embezzlement. Seymour, of course, will be decommissioned immediately. I'm also hugely disappointed in Terry Westen. Did he program this as a little trick? Did Seymour get this idea on his own? The provost will investigate thoroughly.

FRED: I bet the provost plans to investigate without annoying Terry Westen.

MING: That's not our concern. My responsibility is to deal with these infractions at the department level. Professor Warkowski, explain yourself!

SID: That was an official departmental email I got from Seymour. I assumed I had permission to invest.

MING: Permission to invest University funds? You had very little reason for making that assumption.

SID: Maybe so, but Seymour is right. It's great to get some travel money, but that doesn't change the fact that my salary is very low. I had a chance to change my financial situation, and I took it.

MARY: So you withdrew your paper from the conference program?

SID nods.

MARY: Did you consider how that reflects on our department?

SID: I wanted the money!

MING: Professor Brennan.

FRED: I invested my travel allocation, just as Seymour advised. But I didn't bail on my conference. I spent my own money. So, the University wasn't cheated out of anything.

MING: Well, that's not as bad as what Sid did. But it's still totally illegal.

FRED: We were all told to trust Seymour. So, I trusted Seymour.

MING: Emma, I take it you chose not to invest. You made the ethical decision. Applied human values. You were not seduced by a soulless mechanism offering get-rich-quick money.

EMMA: That's right. I didn't think for one second about investing University money with Seymour.

MING: Mary?

MARY: It wasn't hard for me to follow the rules. But I'm a full-professor, and I'm unattached. I don't have to support three kids on an assistant professor's salary.

MING: What a sorry spectacle this is! The five faculty members who invested money with Seymour could be terminated for cause—except that a case can be made—a weak case—that the University somehow authorized the investment option. Therefore, the penalty will be mild, considering the infraction. Those who did not attend the conferences for which they received travel money are ineligible for any kind of professional development support—including course releases and sabbaticals—for 5 years. Those who attended their conference are ineligible for professional development support for 3 years.

FRED: Ming, I'd like to make a brief statement on behalf of the Seymour investors.

MING: I assume this is an apology. Go ahead.

> FRED glances to SID, who nods in recognition of the statement FRED is about to make. Then, as FRED speaks, there is growing astonishment. EMMA and MARY are delighted. MING appears puzzled and ambivalent.

FRED: The Seymour Investors are pleased to announce our own million-dollar contribution to the professional development endowment. With 2 million in travel money, all travel money requests, from both faculty and Ph.D. students, can now be fully funded.

> MARY, EMMA, and MING are amazed. SID smiles.

FRED: Seymour is every bit as good at investing as he is at allocating travel money. Not only can the Seymour Investors now live comfortably, we're in a position to give back to the department.

MARY: Fantastic! Seymour is amazing!

FRED: *(Chuckling.)* Seymour sees more.

EMMA: I hope the rest of us will be able to use Seymour's investment advice.

MING: Emma, I know this university very well, and I strongly suspect this department will never have access to Seymour again. The University will try like hell to adapt Seymour for its own purposes, like managing its endowment funds. You can say good-bye to Seymour.

SID: Yep! That's how it works around here. Faculty get a good thing, and the administration takes it away.

FRED: And that's exactly the kind of thing that would piss off Terry Westen. He built Seymour for *us*. His friend's mother studied in *our* department. Ming, you've gotten to know Westen. Perhaps you and he could have a little conversation where you paint us as underdogs being bullied and cheated by the Central Administration.

MARY: Don't forget to mention the Seymour investors chose to share their good fortune with their colleagues.

MING: *(Slyly.)* Some kind of informal communication might be possible.

FRED: I feel a wave of optimism washing over me. When the administration starts playing with Seymour, he's going dark. But we'll get a new Seymour, a Seymour the university's bureaucrats can't get their greedy fingers on. The new Seymour won't know a thing about travel money. That's no longer a problem. Instead, he'll see to the financial well-being of the faculty in this chronically underpaid department.

SID: Yes. This will be the Seymour that *does more.*

The End

Postscript to "Travel Money"

"Travel Money" is a cheerfully subversive play. We never learn whether Terry Westen intended the investment option or whether Seymour somehow devised it. Either way, we appreciate this violation of the university's regulations, and we hope that Fred's prediction of a new Seymour comes to pass. Furthermore, while we respect the faculty members who refused to break the rules, we also respect the Seymour Investors.

Ming's response to the Seymour Investors is initially conventional and bureaucratic. She is seemingly unmoved by Sid's cynical observation that the university, motivated by financial considerations, will avoid displeasing a billionaire donor. However, Ming has a change of heart. Aligning herself with her faculty colleagues, she hints strongly that when university administrators take control of Seymour, she will tell Terry Westen that the underdog faculty members have been bullied. In Fred's projection of the future, these feisty professors and a bad boy of the software world will foil the agenda of the corporate university.

The Day of the Deal

A 10-minute play by

David K. Farkas

Characters:

Ruth: A young woman and a Ph.D. student in Medieval Studies. From a working-class family. At the beginning of the play, she is heard (voice only) as a deceased woman looking back on her life and, in particular, the day she and her boyfriend Walter decided to get married.

Walter: A young man and a Ph.D. student in Medieval Studies. From a very wealthy family. Ruth's live-in boyfriend. At the beginning of the play, he is heard (voice only) as a deceased man looking back on his life and, in particular, the day that he and Ruth decided to get married.

Ruth and Walter's Middle-aged Daughter (voice-over). Along with her brother, engages in a dialogue with their deceased parents.

Ruth and Walter's Middle-aged Son (voice-over). In his late 30s. Along with his sister, engages in a dialogue with their deceased parents.

Suggested minimum casting:

Ruth. Also plays Middle-Aged Daughter.

Walter. Also plays Middle-Aged Son.

Setting:

It is 1973. In Ruth and Walter's apartment there is a desk with a typewriter, scholarly books, and many typed pages. Some are clipped together in batches, some are in file folders, and some are loose. Others are on the floor. There is a large, very full bookshelf made of unfinished boards and cinder blocks. There is also a small dining room table.

[Scene 1]

> From behind a screen, we hear RUTH and WALTER'S middle-aged son and daughter speaking about their deceased parents—and RUTH and WALTER'S response.

DAUGHTER: We really don't know about The Day of the Deal.

SON: No. And we never will. They took that little story right to the grave.

DAUGHTER: When they talked about their early lives together, the phrase would come up. When one of them uttered it, they would just smile. But it was never a comfortable smile.

SON: Then they would say a few things—always cryptic—and we'd be locked out of their conversation.

DAUGHTER: Very annoying really . . . It would go something like this:

DAUGHTER, speaking as her mother Ruth: "The Day of the Deal. That's when it all changed."

SON, speaking as his father: "Yes, our whole lives. It was 1973. It had gotten rough for us."

DAUGHTER, speaking as her mother: "There never was a day when we saw each other more clearly."

SON: And that would be it. You couldn't get a word more from them. The Day of the Deal was a little black box that they'd never open for us.

RUTH AS OLD WOMAN: *(Sharply to SON.)* Get over it! There's no rule that says parents need to share everything with their kids.

WALTER AS OLD MAN: That's right! We were loving parents. This was always a happy family. But there were good reasons why we never explained "The Day of the Deal."

> The actor playing RUTH appears, carelessly dressed. She sits at the desk and goes into character. RUTH types, stops to think, and resumes typing. She does not look happy. WALTER, handsome and well dressed, appears, holding a carefully wrapped package. RUTH turns her chair to face him. WALTER sets the package down on the table.

WALTER: It's here.

RUTH: I can see.

WALTER: You sound resentful. You can't keep it out of your voice. Couldn't you hide it, just a little? At least right now when I'm opening the package?

RUTH: I am resentful. Why should I hide my feelings? This is *your* big opportunity, not mine. *You* will get a tenure-track position at a good university. I surely will not. Are you a better scholar than me? Hardly. Are you the best Ph.D. student in the department? No. Your family's money has purchased your success.

WALTER: Money buys things of value. That's what money is. That's what money does. Would it be better if I'd bought a Maserati?

RUTH: You could drive around like a fiend in your Maserati, but it wouldn't put you head and shoulders above every doctoral student in the country working in Arthurian romance.

WALTER: I did nothing wrong. The Sunderland Family was ready to sell the manuscript. I agreed to their price and bought it. I will also pay for the transcription. Every medievalist will welcome the publication of *Gawain's Vision*. Then I'll donate the manuscript to a university library so that any scholar can examine it.

RUTH: Yes, but you will be the editor of the definitive edition, and you will have the first opportunity to write an interpretive essay. My dissertation is very good Arthurian scholarship, with some new ideas. But I'll be lucky to get a job teaching freshman comp and sophomore survey in someplace like Enid, Oklahoma. I'll be in Enid, and you'll be at Princeton, or somewhere like that, teaching graduate seminars.

WALTER: Ruth, we always knew a time would come when we'd go on separate paths. We love each other. We've been happy together for two years in this apartment. But the endgame was always here, every day, sitting silently with us at dinner. You will get your Ph.D. I will get mine, and the odds of us getting jobs anywhere near each other are very slim. If we were regular people, with regular career plans, we'd probably be married. I certainly would have proposed.

RUTH: So open the damn package.

[Scene 2]

RUTH and WALTER, dressed differently than in Scene 1, are standing and facing each other in the apartment. The papers on RUTH's desk and some of the furnishings are somewhat re-arranged to suggest the passage of time.

WALTER: We need to talk.

RUTH: What about?

WALTER: You know what about. Something has been wrong, very wrong, since you got back from the Medieval Studies Conference. Something happened there. I don't know what.

RUTH: It was a bad conference for me—that's all.

WALTER: No. You *expected* it to be a bad conference for you. It's something more. Much more. It's changed everything. It's changed things in bed. We've never had that problem before. What happened at the conference?

RUTH: Nothing happened!

WALTER: Nothing? I *know* something happened. You need to tell me, Ruth.

RUTH breaks down into tears. She is half hysterical.

RUTH: I wanted my chance. So I did something. We are not married.

WALTER: What?

RUTH: I met a man. He said he was an acquisitions editor at the Indiana University Press. He said he works on their Medieval Studies series. He'd read my book proposal—the summary, the first chapter, the reviewers' letters. He talked like an editor. He had a business card.

WALTER: Oh, God!

RUTH: He said my dissertation was excellent work, totally suitable for the series. But there were two other proposals that were equally good, and they're only looking for one manuscript this year. An hour in his hotel room would tip the balance. I did it, Walter. One hour, just one hour. It was stupid.

WALTER: Fuck! Fuck! So, what happened after?

RUTH: When I followed up, the press told me there was no such acquisitions editor. No one with that name. No one who matched my description of the guy. I sold myself. And I sold myself like a fool.

WALTER: I can hardly believe this.

RUTH: Believe it. I did it. If the sexiest man in America had his eyes on me, I'd have said no in one second. For me, this had nothing to do with sex. It had to do with not wasting six years in graduate school. Not having to be a total failure. Not having to explain to my parents that everything I've done, everything they've done to help me, was basically for nothing. I'm sorry, so very sorry. But you can understand this, Walter.

WALTER: You're so sorry. But you wouldn't have been sorry if the guy was for real and you were getting your dissertation published. Then how would you have felt about the conference? You might have been sitting around the apartment smiling this past week.

RUTH: I don't know. I'm not gonna know. When he was talking, I was thinking about having a book on my vita—University of Indiana Press. Medieval Studies Series. Not about much else. There wasn't a lot of time for me to think into the future. It was do it or don't do it.

WALTER: Well, you did it. You were a kind of prostitute.

RUTH: I'm not saying what I was. How did he get my book proposal? It's gone to just a handful of university presses. In the Department, only my committee has seen it.

WALTER: That's not exactly what matters here.

RUTH: I wanted a chance to get what you always get, what you get without any trouble at all. Maybe you shouldn't be so quick to judge. I've been teaching two sections of comp every quarter. You've sailed through the program because you teach just one section a year—just enough to put teaching experience on your vita. I'm three years older than you, but with your money, you're as far along as I am. As an undergraduate, I struggled every year to pay my tuition. You've never struggled at anything. And remember, we are not married. It's not the same when you're not married. I needed to plan for my future—a future without you.

WALTER: A fine job you made of it . . . I need to think. I'm going out. I'm not judging you. Yes, of course I am. But I need to think.

RUTH: Walter. . .

WALTER abruptly exits the apartment.

[Scene 3]

RUTH is sitting at her chair, but it is turned away from her desk. She is distraught. WALTER enters. RUTH looks up, fearfully.

RUTH: Walter? . . .

WALTER: Ruth. I did a lot of thinking.

RUTH: And? . . .

WALTER: I've got a deal for you. I come from a business family. We make deals.

RUTH: This is a time for a deal?

WALTER: Today, yes . . . First, you marry me. Second, I forget about what happened at the conference. Not quite "forget," but let it go. That will not be easy. Third, *Gawain's Vision* is yours. You get to edit it. You write the articles. Deep down, you're more the scholar than I am. I have other options. Wherever you get your teaching job, they'll be a law school not too far away. My mind is suited just as well for law as for scholarship. With my family connections, I'll have opportunities in law— one way or another.

RUTH: You call this a deal? This is a gift. This is beyond what I could have wished for. Very few men would do all this, Walter. Yes, yes, I'll marry you. We've both wanted it.

RUTH moves close to kiss WALTER. With a smile and a light-hearted gesture, he stops her.

WALTER: Wait a minute. You've only heard half of the deal. There are two things I want you to give me.

RUTH: Yes.

WALTER: I'm sick and tired of being reminded all the time about my privilege, my family, my money. A big piece of my privilege is now going to you.

RUTH: Maybe it's wrong for me to take the manuscript, to get to the head of the line. But the manuscript is here, and I *want* it. You know very well what I was willing to do to be a real professor.

WALTER: Yes, and I understand. I can forgive that. While I was out walking, I realized that we *do* need to stay together. And you do need to become a scholar at a serious university. I want you to feel OK about editing *Gawain's Vision*. You didn't buy it. I did.

RUTH: We've certainly balanced out the privilege. I have no more right to complain. I have no more resentment. Thank you, Walter.

> RUTH moves close to kiss WALTER. Once again, with a smile and a light-hearted gesture, he stops her.

WALTER: Wait a minute . . . Remember, Ruth, there's a *second* part to this deal—something else I'm asking for.

RUTH: Whatever it is, I think I'll be fine with it.

WALTER: Wherever we go, wherever you get your teaching job, we're going to live the way I'm comfortable, the way I grew up. No more cinder block bookshelves. Now it's mahogany. We'll buy a big house in the nicest section of town. Yes, tasteful and all. But very nice. Wherever you get your job, we'll be members of the best country club. The best of everything. I can only imagine how this will go down with your English department colleagues.

RUTH: I know what you mean. It won't be pretty.

WALTER: If you want to drive to campus in a 15-year-old Chevy, go right ahead. But that's not what I'll be driving, and that's not what we'll be in when we go out to dinner on Saturday night.

RUTH: Fair is fair. More than fair. You've given up a lot. I will give you every bit of what you're asking for—with a willing and loving heart.

> RUTH moves close to kiss WALTER. He joins her in a joyful kiss.

WALTER: I love you, Ruth. There was never any doubt about that. And I'll be very pleased to be married to the distinguished editor of *Gawain's Vision*.

RUTH: Walter, it's been hard thinking about what was going to happen when we finished our degrees. Then there was the conference. Today everything really fell apart, but you rescued us. This is the day you asked me to marry you. But it's something else as well. It's the Day of the Deal.

The End

Postscript to "The Day of the Deal"

The cruel academic job market in the humanities is the background for this story about a loving relationship that survives—indeed, more than survives—a crisis. The crisis is resolved by Walter's forgiveness and extreme generosity. Although the Day of the Deal is a pivotal and hugely positive moment in Walter and Ruth's lives together, there is nothing in the underlying situation for Ruth to be proud of. It is very clear why they kept this story from their children.

The story derives from factual circumstances. First, I knew several English graduate students (and junior-level instructors) who decided that their ability to closely analyze and argue about literary texts was applicable to a career in law and who therefore made the change. Also, I know of a wealthy scholar who purchased the only extant manuscript of an obscure but significant work of medieval literature. He then greatly advanced his academic career by publishing the first scholarly edition. Finally, the deception that took place at the conference closely follows an actual event. Sometime in the early 70's, a man claiming to be an acquisitions editor for a university press (I vaguely recall that it was the University of Indiana) bedded several female graduate students during an MLA (Modern Language Association) conference. He was never found or identified. I read an account of this in either (or both) *The Chronicle of Higher Education* or the *New York Times*. Also, I believe that some kind of after-the-fact warning was issued by the MLA.

Closer to home, a female Ph.D. student (young and physically attractive) in my cohort in the English department at the University of Minnesota was one of the women approached by this man. She told a group of us that he had somehow learned about her dissertation (not impossible because job candidates often sent dissertation summaries and chapters to schools that show some interest in hiring them). She also revealed, with surprising candor, I thought, that she had very nearly accepted his offer to publish her dissertation in return for sex but had decided to remain faithful to her husband.

Wasserman the Water Man

A 10-minute play by

David K. Farkas

I place this play in the public domain. Anyone is welcome to distribute, perform, modify, or expand upon the script of this play. – David K. Farkas, 2020.

Setting:
Buildings on the campus of a mid-size university in a mid-size city in New York State.

Characters:
Seth Wasserman: A college student.

Roger, Aaron, and **Katie:** College students and friends of Seth.

Dr. Lewis: A faculty member in the chemistry department (any gender).

Narrator: Can be played by "Dr. Lewis."

[Scene 1]

> The NARRATOR enters.

NARRATOR: It is the year 1966, on the campus of Masconig University, located in the city of Masconig, in Central New York State. Roger, Aaron, Katie, and Seth are second-year students who have returned to campus for spring semester after the winter break.

> The NARRATOR exits. AARON, ROGER, and KATIE enter.

AARON: Seth dropped out of pre-med. He must have flunked the final in Chordate Anatomy.

ROGER: I thought he was doing OK in Chordate.

KATIE: Me too. His GPA is high.

ROGER: He didn't have any trouble with Organic Chemistry.

AARON: Well, I heard he dropped pre-med.

SETH enters.

ROGER: Hey, Wasserman. Did you drop out of pre-med?

SETH: Yes.

ROGER: Why?!

SETH: I don't want to be a doctor.

AARON: What? You're a Jewish guy from New York City, and you don't want to be a doctor? New York Jews *wash* out of pre-med. They don't *drop* out if they are doing well in their classes.

ROGER: Your parents having financial problems? There are always loans—even for med school.

SETH: Nothing like that. I decided I don't want to be a doctor.

AARON: You gonna be a pharmaceutical salesman?

ROGER: A folksinger?

KATIE: Why are you guys making so much trouble for Seth? . . . *(In a studied tone of voice.)* Seth, I'd be interested in hearing why you're no longer interested in a medical career and what your current plans might be.

SETH: I'm going to study ecology. I'm going to help protect the environment.

AARON: What's ecology?

ROGER: Dumbass, it's the study of "eeks." Eek-ology. But Seth, what are eeks? Do we have any eeks in New York State?

KATIE: Roger, you're the dumbass.

SETH: Ecology means how natural and man-made systems interact, how they fit together. In particular, I'm looking at how industrialization is harming the environment.

AARON: What environment?

SETH: Like what's all around us—the air, the water. Water pollution is becoming a terrible problem. Air pollution, too.

ROGER: Doesn't that stuff just take care of itself?

KATIE: Seth, do you mean something like "conservation"?

SETH: Kinda. But "conservation" is an old-fashioned term. It doesn't get at how one problem is tied to another problem. Ecology is a systems approach.

KATIE: Do they even teach that here?

SETH: No, not really. Officially, I'll be a chemistry major. I'll be working a lot with Dr. Lewis and Dr. Hamid—they're the department's water chemists. Dr. Lewis is especially interested in ecology. I got interested in it when my T.A. in Organic Chemistry told me about her work. So, I dropped in at her office hours, and we started talking. I'll do some independent studies courses with them. I'll take biology courses. There are two systems engineering courses in the Industrial Engineering department that I can take. I'll need statistics. Maybe a course or two in political science. Then, I'll be ready to work as an ecologist.

AARON: Is this any kind of paid work?

SETH: I hope so. Maybe big companies will want to hire ecologists to help them understand how their operations affect the environment. Maybe government. I don't exactly know.

ROGER: Well, maybe ecology can be your side gig. You can support your family as a folksinger.

AARON: Have you told your parents yet?

SETH: Yep. That's what winter break was all about in the Wasserman household. Arguing with me, pleading with me—every day I was home. It was tag-team: First my dad. Then my mom. Then my dad again. When they weren't arguing with me, they walked around the house like someone had just died.

AARON: I sure wouldn't want to take that bit of news home. "Mom, Dad, I hate to shatter all your hopes and dreams—but I'm not going to be a doctor like you were planning on since I was a child."

AARON pretends to be SETH'S father. Full of grief, he addresses KATIE, as though she were his wife.

AARON: "He doesn't want to be a doctor! And he's always been a smart boy. What did we do wrong?"

SETH: That's about the picture.

ROGER: Man, it's tough for Jews, for the guys anyway. Whatever major I decide on, my parents won't think too much about it.

KATIE: Do Jewish women get a pass on this craziness?

AARON: No way! For the women, it's *marry* a doctor.

ROGER: You know, "the times they are a-changing." Maybe in a few years all those Jewish women will be looking to marry an ecologist. Seth, you'll have more girls than you can handle.

SETH: I don't think I should count on that.

KATIE: Well, whatever the Jewish women decide about marrying ecologists, I think it's great that Seth has his own idea for what he wants to do and that he's going after it

[Scene 2]

SETH and KATIE, with textbooks and wire-bound notebooks, are studying. Two other chairs are vacant. SETH has a cup of coffee. He also has two quart-size jars full of dirty water with sediment and debris visible at the bottom. AARON and ROGER enter.

AARON: Hi, Seth . . . Hey, Katie.

KATIE: Hi.

ROGER: You guys up for a study break? If not, we'll move right along.

SETH: A study break sounds good. Grab a seat.

AARON and ROGER sit. They can't help but notice the two jars.

ROGER: What's that?

SETH: Water samples from the Masconig. I filled one jar upstream of the International Polymer plant and the other about 100 yards downstream of IP. There are pollutants in the first sample, but there's much worse stuff in the downstream sample. So all those pipes going into the river from the plant are polluting the river. Also, I talked to a few guys who work there. I'm learning about how much stuff they pump into the river.

ROGER: What's the big deal? No one fishes in that river. Doesn't it all wash out to the ocean anyway?

SETH: Maybe people *could* fish in the Masconig. The Indians sure did. Maybe people could swim in the river someday. Anyway, the chemicals

84

flow from the Masconig all the way down the Hudson and into the ocean. And it's not just the water. Animals eat the fish and drink the water. Pollutants get into the soil.

AARON: Well, that man's an ecologist. What do you think about all this, Katie?

KATIE: Maybe fighting for the environment is like political activism. If wars kill people, so does pollution—just slower, and you can't see it. If we protest to achieve social justice, we can fight for a better environment.

ROGER: *(Ironically.)* Oh. Yeah! You go to the SDS folks with that. They'll love it. Forget Vietnam. Forget Civil Rights. What we really need to protest is dirty water.

SETH: The connection between the environment and social justice isn't that far-fetched. Political activists might listen to environmentalists someday.

[Scene 3]

SETH sits across from DR. LEWIS in his faculty office.

DR. LEWIS: I'm sorry, Seth, but I have bad news for you. Your independent studies plan was not approved.

SETH: What?

DR. LEWIS: I heard from Dr. Johnson. It's definite. International Polymer found out about your research, and someone from IP talked to Johnson. This department would barely exist if we didn't get money—all kinds of money—from IP. From other companies too, but a whole lot from IP.

SETH: I've put in a lot of work on this project. I was counting on those credits.

DR. LEWIS: I'm so sorry, Seth. I didn't see this coming.

SETH: What should I do, Dr. Lewis?

DR. LEWIS: I don't know.

SETH thinks hard and gathers his resolution.

SETH: I do. I'm going to finish the project. Credits or no credits . . . No one is going to stop me from working in the lab—are they?

DR. LEWIS: You're not supposed to be doing unauthorized work in the lab. But I'm way too busy to notice who's doing what. Keep a low profile. If you need help with the stats, we can talk.

SETH: Thanks, Dr. Lewis. I want my research to make a difference. I'm going to make that happen.

DR. LEWIS: Seth, I don't think you see the difficulties here. In a rudimentary way, your data make a strong case. But no journal will publish this. The reviewers will say, "You've shown that a study should be done." A publishable study would require much more extensive data collection, river flow measurements, a more complete chemical analysis—things no undergraduate can do. And no one in this department—not Dr. Hamid, not me, not anyone—is going to buck the chair and help you turn your bottles of water into a research publication. I'm sorry, Seth. That's just how it is.

SETH: If the research is basically sound, I can go to the newspapers with it.

DR. LEWIS: Maybe, but International Polymer is all over this town. Newspaper exposé? I don't think it's gonna happen . . . Seth, the environmental movement is just beginning. Someday we'll be able to take on big corporations. Someday people will listen to us. But that's going to be years from now. If this is what you want to do with your life, you need to be ready for opposition, for disappointments. Do you understand? Are you ready for all that?

SETH: Dr. Lewis, I can handle anything.

DR. LEWIS: You can? How do you know that?

SETH: When I switched from pre-med to ecology, I fought with my parents all through winter break. They love me, but it was the biggest blow-up we ever had. Then, there were family friends—people who've known me all my life . . .

> SETH stands, stretches his body, and then looks down at an imaginary SETH in his chair. He pokes emphatically with his forefinger.

SETH: "Seth, once you give up pre-med, you'll never get another chance at medicine. In a few years this environmental thing may be forgotten, then what? Don't ruin your life, boy" . . . Then it was my relatives when the family got together over the holidays. Even my Uncle Irving, who sorts mail for the Post Office, knows better than me what I should study in college. After hearing from my mom that I don't want to be a doctor, my aunts didn't want to look straight at me. It was painful, Dr. Lewis. But here I am. You might say I'm already a battle-hardened ecologist.

DR. LEWIS: As bad as that! At war with your whole family? Wow!

SETH: Yes. Except for my grandmother.

DR. LEWIS: Your grandmother. What did she say?

SETH: With everyone giving me grief, she took me aside. She said, "'Wasserman.' In Yiddish that means 'water man.' Maybe there's some significance to that. Maybe this is what you were meant to do."

DR LEWIS: What did you say to her?

SETH: Nothing. I just kissed her. She's right, of course. I know my future—Wasserman, the Water Man.

The End

Postscript to "Wasserman the Water Man"

"Wasserman the Water Man" looks at issues that loom large in the lives of undergraduate students: What courses to take, what career paths to pursue, and, in some instances, explaining and even defending their choices to family and friends. When I taught at West Virginia University, I encountered students whose parents and relatives had not wanted them to attend college or who were deeply ambivalent. These families expected (with good cause) that their college graduate would now be culturally different from them and might very well choose to live far from where they were raised. When I taught at Texas Tech, there were many students who learned no-till farming and other modern agricultural techniques in their courses. Now they were seriously at odds with their parents, who remained committed to older farming and ranching practices. "We saved our dollars to send Billy Joe to Tech, and now he just causes trouble around here!"

"Wasserman the Water Man" takes place in 1966 at a New York State university with many Jewish students. Not surprisingly, therefore, these educational and career conflicts revolve around the deep-rooted Jewish fixation with a career in medicine. I know this territory well. Many years ago, I grievously disappointed my parents by announcing that I was going to switch my major from biology/pre-med to English, an area of study I didn't even know existed until I arrived on campus. For more on the Jewish context of this play, you can read the postscript to "Wasserman the Water Man" in my collection *Fourteen Jewish Flavored 10-Minute Plays* (Amazon/Kindle, 2022).

I wrote this play for the campaign kickoff of a city council candidate in the Seattle suburb of Lake Forest Park, where I live. The candidate, Dr. Tracy Furutani, is a university faculty member with a strong commitment to protecting the environment. Quite remarkably, a Jewish pre-med student and his non-Jewish fiancé played Seth and Katie. Tracy played Dr. Lewis and was addressed as "Dr. Furutani" in our performance. I played Aaron. It all went over well—plus Tracy was elected!

While the play is about student life, Jewish culture, and the environmental movement, a part of the plot turns on the pernicious influence of corporate money. When International Polymer seeks to stop Seth's research, the chair of the chemistry department surrenders. Dr. Lewis deserves credit for her willingness to help Seth surreptitiously, but neither Dr. Lewis nor Dr. Hamid are willing to confront the chair or publicly protest his actions. Furthermore, the local newspaper cannot be counted on for independent journalism. They too are intimidated by the city's biggest employer. Seth himself, however, is strong-willed and remains fully committed to his ideals.

Academic Misconduct

A 10-minute play by

David K. Farkas

Characters:

Stephen: An undergraduate English major.

Johanna: An undergraduate student.

Dr. Jerome Foster: Chair of the English department. He is formal and bureaucratic.

Dr. Carson Adams: Director of English composition. Any gender. Carson is informal and empathetic.

Setting:

The spacious faculty office of Dr. Foster. There is a desk and a coffee table. Foster, Adams, and Stephen are seated around the table. Backstage is a door that opens to the anteroom of Foster's office, where a receptionist/secretary—who is never seen—is working.

DR. FOSTER: Thank you, Stephen, for coming to talk with us. Dr. Adams and I want to emphasize that you've done nothing wrong. This isn't about plagiarism or any kind of academic misconduct.

STEPHEN: But Ms. Estevez *did* talk to Dr. Adams about my writing assignment, and Dr. Adams *did* come to you. So, obviously, something is bothering you folks.

DR. FOSTER: Well . . . Perhaps there's a potential problem. Something to do with . . . how well you are doing as a student. Whether or not you are thriving here.

STEPHEN: *(With a sardonic chuckle.)* "Thriving"?

DR. FOSTER: Yes. This may be a large university, but we truly want every student to thrive.

STEPHEN: Does *anybody* around here "thrive"? Do *you* thrive, Dr. Foster?

    Annoyed, FOSTER ignores STEPHEN'S comment.

DR. FOSTER: There is a problem we need to deal with, which is why we're having this meeting.

DR. ADAMS: Camilla Estevez was concerned because of the content of your final assignment. Your paper depicts acts of violence on a university campus. Camilla is a teaching assistant, and she spoke to *me* because I direct the writing program.

STEPHEN: Your concern is what's written in a paper?

DR. FOSTER: Yes. We draw a distinction between student work with violent content and student work that suggests violent behavior. In this instance . . .

STEPHEN: You think I'm emotionally unstable. A violent person. A threat.

DR. FOSTER: We have legitimate concerns, very legitimate concerns, about your safety and the safety of the campus community. According to University guidelines, we are fully justified in calling for an immediate intervention by Campus Security. Dr. Adams, however, suggested a different course of action—which is why we are talking with you. We hope that the three of us can resolve this issue informally. Ms. Estevez was not invited because, while she teaches for us, she is, in fact, a student, a graduate student.

STEPHEN: OK. OK. I get it. Actually, I'm glad she's not here.

    STEPHEN looks at his watch.

STEPHEN: What did she say about me?

DR. ADAMS: She respects your intellect. She likes the way you add new ideas, new perspectives, to class discussion. She likes you, as a person.

STEPHEN: I like her. The whole class does.

DR. FOSTER: Perhaps we're moving away from the matter at hand. We need to focus on the paper, and what it suggests about your emotional health and potential for violent behavior.

DR. ADAMS: I think what Dr. Foster is suggesting is that it's not unusual for people—at any age—to feel overwhelmed by . . .

STEPHEN: I'm not overwhelmed.

DR. ADAMS: People carry secret, unseen wounds. Things that have happened to . . .

STEPHEN: I understand what you're talking about. But I don't have big psychological problems. Anyway, I can get psychological counseling any time I want. It's part of the student health plan I pay for.

DR. FOSTER: So, you are saying you do not have psychological problems, that we have no reason for concern.

STEPHEN: I don't have psychological problems. The *world* has big problems, and there's plenty of reason for concern. Don't you have concerns about the world, Dr. Foster?

DR. FOSTER: Of course, I do.

STEPHEN: Doesn't it all get to you sometimes? Climate change. Constant famine—children starving to death every day. Brutal wars. Moral indifference. People just going through their days essentially ignoring everything around them. Doesn't that concern you, Dr. Foster? What about you, Dr. Adams?

DR. ADAMS: Yes, but I try not to give in to despair. That just cripples us.

DR. FOSTER: Many people share your concerns, Stephen. Faculty as well as students. But not everyone submits a paper depicting horrific violence.

STEPHEN: It was just an English paper. A piece of writing. An assignment I turned in.

DR. ADAMS: Yes. Yes.

STEPHEN is becoming agitated. Again, he looks at his watch.

STEPHEN: Writing is about using your imagination to explore your world. We're encouraged to do that. I have friends in some of the creative writing courses who write stories that are very dark, violent even. And there are famous writers—Joyce Carol Oates, for instance. Her work is full of violence, perversion, everything.

DR. FOSTER: *(Surprised and impressed.)* You know Joyce Carol Oates?

STEPHEN: She's one of my favorite contemporary authors.

DR. ADAMS: *(To DR. FOSTER.)* Stephen has done excellent work all through the quarter. I'm not surprised that he's a serious reader.

DR. FOSTER: Who else do you read?

STEPHEN: Ian McEwan, Sherman Alexi, Margaret Atwood, Toni Morrison. There are others.

DR. FOSTER: Stephen, you're certainly right about the importance of the literary imagination. And—of course—we want our students to feel free to write papers on any topic that interests them . . . But you're in a first-year composition course, not creative writing. And the topic of the class assignment was "How I Envision My Future." Also, the assignment was supposed to be 750 words, and you wrote—something like . . . *(Glances at DR. ADAMS for confirmation.)* 15 pages?

STEPHEN: I really got into it. I don't believe that the syllabus specifies a maximum length for the assignment, just a minimum.

> DR. FOSTER and DR. ADAMS exchange glances that make clear they are satisfied with STEPHEN'S responses.

DR. FOSTER: Stephen, you are obviously a very bright young man. And very articulate, with an understanding of literature and the creative imagination. There is the fact that you submitted your paper in a composition course, not in a creative writing course, where this kind of writing is more expected. But, we are impressed by the way you have clarified your intentions. I think our concerns have been alleviated.

STEPHEN: OK. I wouldn't want you folks to have any concerns.

> STEPHEN looks again at his watch.

DR. FOSTER: But we *are* going to ask you to submit another paper. I don't believe that a paper that depicts extreme violence on a university campus should be accepted as coursework.

> ADAMS glances sharply at FOSTER to express his disagreement with this requirement. STEPHEN notices.

STEPHEN: There's not going to be another paper, Dr. Foster.

DR. ADAMS: Stephen, I think you can understand why Dr. Foster wants a different paper. I know you can easily write 750 words.

DR. FOSTER: You are not enrolled in a creative writing course. You were assigned a factual paper on how you envision your future. Therefore, you did not fulfill the assignment.

STEPHEN: I see. It's a question of factuality. But it's never really definite what is and isn't factual. Perhaps my paper is very factual.

DR. ADAMS: You can think of the new paper as an opportunity for you to further explore your ideas, your emotions. We can be flexible about the due date. Especially . . . given the stress this whole situation has caused for you.

STEPHEN: There is not going to be another paper. *(Laughs.)* I have one more thing to tell you. I *am* guilty of "academic misconduct." My girlfriend, Johanna, helped me write the paper. Some parts we wrote together. A few pages she wrote herself—with me looking on. Despite your rules, it made sense for us to work together on "How I Envision My Future." We envision the same future.

DR. ADAMS: *(With some enthusiasm.)* Are you and Johanna engaged?

STEPHEN: That would be a no. We're not that optimistic about the future.

DR. FOSTER: I'm disappointed. You know that you are required to complete all assignments independently. The English department responds seriously to all instances of cheating. You are actually fortunate that we didn't accept the paper as a course assignment. For that reason, we don't need to take this case to the Board of Student Conduct.

> STEPHEN looks at his watch, withdraws into his own thoughts, then turns his attention back to DR FOSTER and DR. ADAMS.

STEPHEN: *(Laughing sardonically.)* "Board of Student Conduct"! I believe we've moved way, way beyond the Board of Student Conduct. And, the *(Paraphrasing the earlier words of DR. ADAMS.)* "stress this situation has caused me"? That's insignificant. Life can get a whole lot more stressful . . . I am about to demonstrate this. By the way, Ms. Estevez is a good instructor. None of this is because of her.

DR. FOSTER: What are you saying, Stephen?

> STEPHEN rises as if to leave.

DR. ADAMS: Stephen?

> STEPHEN opens the office door. In steps JOHANNA. She is properly dressed, in a skirt and a blazer (or buttoned sweater). But she has a pistol lightly taped to the inside of the garment, and she is pulling it loose as she enters the office. In her other hand is some kind of a paper form. She points the gun menacingly at both DR. FOSTER and DR. ADAMS. STEPHEN rises and stands beside her.

STEPHEN: This is Johanna. Co-author of "How I Envision My Future."

> STEPHEN gestures toward the gun held in JOHANNA'S extended arm.

Here it is—my future. Johanna's too. And you're the lucky folks who get to share in it. Dr. Foster, you definitely should not have called me into your office.

JOHANNA: Definitely a mistake!

DR. FOSTER: My God!

DR. ADAMS: Stephen! Don't do anything. Johanna!

STEPHEN: Just like in my paper, Johanna and I have decided to put a little shudder of fear into that giant ball of shit which is the universe. Wake people up to how things are.

> STEPHEN turns to JOHANNA with a laugh.

STEPHEN: What's that form you have there?

> He leans over to take a look.

STEPHEN: You gonna sign up for an independent studies course?

JOHANNA: I told the secretary that Dr. Foster said I could come into his office to get his signature real quick before his next appointment. She was very nice.

> JOHANNA lets the form drop to the floor.

STEPHEN: Do you want to shoot her?

DR. FOSTER: You're insane! Don't! Please. Don't kill her. Don't kill anyone.

DR. ADAMS: Stephen, Johanna, there's no reason for this. You'll be destroying your own lives.

JOHANNA: What life? What life do I have? What lives do any of us have in this world?

STEPHEN: Our plan is to die along with you. Johanna will fire the final two shots.

> DR. FOSTER springs from his chair to grab the gun from JOHANNA. But she is quick, and he sees that she's just a short moment from pulling the trigger, so he stops.

JOHANNA: *(To DR. FOSTER.)* Sit!

> DR. FOSTER only half-sits. He is considering another attack. But half-sitting is sufficient for JOHANNA not to pull the trigger.

STEPHEN: Should we kill her—the secretary?

JOHANNA: I don't know. I don't see any reason to.

STEPHEN: OK, Jo. That works for me. Professors, I think our meeting is about over.

> JOHANNA lifts the gun as though to shoot DR. FOSTER.

DR. FOSTER and **DR. ADAMS:** No. Please. God! Oh. Oh. Please!

DR. ADAMS: Stephen, what about Camilla Estevez? This will ruin her life.

STEPHEN: She warned Dr. Foster about me, so she's in the clear. I can write a damn note saying she did nothing wrong.

DR. ADAMS: You know better than that. People will blame her. She'll blame herself. She'll carry the guilt forever.

JOHANNA: Stevie, I think we need to get on with this. Do it, or forget it.

DR. FOSTER: You both have parents, families. People who love . . .

STEPHEN: Shut the fuck up please.

JOHANNA: We could just kill Foster.

STEPHEN: That's a half-way measure. Do we want to die or go to prison because we shot Foster? Hardly seems worth it.

DR. ADAMS: *None* of this is worth it. You two are like an airplane pointed straight down in a tailspin. But you can just pull up. You don't need to crash. Do it for Camilla if for no other reason. This is just one crazy moment in your lives. It doesn't need to be anything more than that.

STEPHEN: Johanna, are we just in a tailspin? Can we really pull out? Do we *want* to pull out?

JOHANNA: We did sort of talk ourselves into this. We reached a logical conclusion, and then we went with it. But, I don't know. Lots of our friends feel the same way as we do about the world—and they're not doing crazy shit like this. I'm not against waking up tomorrow morning. Going on with our lives. Maybe we can get our 300 dollars back from the gun shop!

DR. ADAMS: Only four people in the world know anything about this. And they're all in this room.

DR. FOSTER: Carson, what's going on?

DR. ADAMS: *(To STEPHEN and JOHANNA.)* If you say you're done with ideas about killing people, I'll believe you. Foster too. You should live your lives. Make things better. At least try. *(In a tone of finality.)* Nothing happened here today. OK? It was just a Cosmic fart.

DR. FOSTER: Carson, what are you agreeing to?

DR. ADAMS: Jerry, this would be a real good time for you to be quiet.

DR. ADAMS: *(To JOHANNA and STEPHEN).* Did you post anything on social media?

JOHANNA: No. But there's a note in my room. Stephen wrote one too.

DR. ADAMS: OK. That's good. Those notes can disappear.

JOHANNA: If we call this off, Foster will call the police in a second.

DR. FOSTER: I won't! I won't! I promise.

STEPHEN: Do we believe him?

JOHANNA: That would be a no.

DR. ADAMS: Jerry, I say we do this. You need to agree not to call Campus Security or anybody. Not today, not ever. Call it a leap of faith. If they are willing to go on with their lives, we need to let them.

FOSTER looks baffled and uncertain.

STEPHEN: I don't trust Foster.

JOHANNA: Slimy bastard.

DR. ADAMS: You can trust *me* to take care of Foster if he backs out of our deal. I'll swear nothing ever happened. You two just talked about that paper. He was very nervous and had a panic attack. Stuff that you wrote in the paper got into his head . . . Jerry, this is your moment. Time for you to commit. For God's sake, sound like you mean it—and then really *mean* it. Mean it! A leap of faith. A little trust.

JOHANNA: Come on, slime ball.

DR. ADAMS: Jesus, Johanna. That doesn't help any. How's this? Give me that gun. If Jerry turns you in, *I'll* shoot him.

JOHANNA: I like that. The gun is yours.

> JOHANNA hands the gun to ADAMS, who makes a whimsical gesture of shooting FOSTER.

DR. FOSTER: Carson! Have you gone mad?

DR. ADAMS: *(Addressing everyone.)* This whole thing never happened at all. Camilla suggested a talk. We had our little talk. No need to write a new paper, Stephen. Foster will *personally* give you a 4.0 grade *(Whimsically lifting the gun.)*—won't you, Jerry?

> FOSTER is baffled. He lowers his head as if trying to escape from everything around him. Then he lifts his head sorrowfully.

DR. FOSTER: This is more than I can deal with.

DR. ADAMS: You don't have to deal with it at all. Go home. Tell Barbara you had a good day. Then, tonight, you have a terrible dream. So tomorrow you can talk to Barbara about that dream. *This* is that dream. You can see a therapist. Whatever you want. But it was nothing but a bad dream. When you walk out of here at 4:30, give Joan a pleasant good-bye. Like it's been a normal day.

> ADAMS picks up the form and hands it to FOSTER.

DR. ADAMS: Sign it, Jerry. For us, this form has a secret meaning. It is our agreement. It's trust. *(Looks to JOHANNA and STEPHEN.)* No shootings—ever. *(Looks to DR. FOSTER.)* And you never tell anyone, Jerry. All this is just a nightmare you're going to have tonight. Nothing real. You got it? This is your reprieve. Sign the form. Your signature will stand for the agreement we're all making now.

DR. FOSTER: This is insane.

DR. ADAMS: Yeah, that's just how it goes sometimes. *(To STEPHEN and JOHANNA.)* You pulled the plane out of its tailspin. We're all going home.

DR. FOSTER: *(Sounding muddled and confused.)* This is very insane. You don't really know what these two will do.

STEPHEN: We don't know for sure that we can trust *you*.

DR. ADAMS: It's a leap of faith.

FOSTER signs with an air of resignation and compliance.

DR. FOSTER: A leap of faith.

The End

Postscript to "Academic Misconduct"

"Academic Misconduct" looks back at the tragic mass shooting by an undergraduate student at Virginia Tech in 2007. The student had given hints about his murderous intentions in his creative writing papers. But the play skirts tragedy due to the actions of Carson Adams. Showing empathy and creativity, Adams dissolves the homicidal impulse that has taken hold of Stephen and Johanna. Will this be permanent? We do not know. It is a leap of faith. Adams also exhibits forcefulness and psychological insight when he/she/they persuades Dr. Foster to keep quiet about the near murders. We do not know, but it seems likely that Foster will follow through.

At the beginning of the play, both Foster and Adams foolishly set aside their suspicions when Stephen displays his knowledge of literature. The audience sees the disastrous direction in which the interview is headed, but the English professors, blinded by their love of literature, miss obvious clues. Even so, Adams makes an emotional connection with Stephen. Also, Adams takes note of Stephen's fondness for Camilla Estevez, which proves to be the slim opening through which Stephen's sanity re-asserts itself at the last possible moment.

While well intentioned, Foster is cold and bureaucratic. He rigidly fixates, on the requirement that Stephen write a second paper and on Stephen's plagiarism. In contrast, Stephen exhibits a nimble, even playful intellect. Johanna is cut from the same cloth.

Comedy is often built on the contrast between inflexible, rule-bound behavior and spontaneity and freedom from restraint. Foster's clumsy rule-bound behavior adds an element of comedy. It also proves fortunate for the outcome of the play. Stephen and Johanna find it easier to relate to Adams when they see the contrast between Adams and Foster.

The risk that Adams and Foster take in agreeing not to call the police recalls the risk taken by Paul Rogers in not having the Minneapolis police arrest Jim Thompson. We will see this kind of risk-taking one more time in "Professor Jim."

In 2019, Jean Farkas and I organized the Goat Hill Theater, a group of friends based in Lake Forest Park, Washington, who perform our own 10-minute plays before an audience of friends. Here is the YouTub link to "Academic Misconduct":
https://youtu.be/wDeuGb6rdfQ

Margaret Reynolds Enters Heaven

A 10-minute play by

David K. Farkas

Characters:

Sandra McKnight: Editor

Arthur Warrington: Editor

Lucinda Brodeur: Editor

Margaret Reynolds: Head Editor

Jean Farber: Proofreader

St. Peter: Keeper of the Gates of Heaven

Narrator

Suggested minimum casting:

Jean

Margaret

Arthur/St. Peter

"Lucinda" or "Sandra" can double as Jean. The actor who doesn't double as Jean can play the Narrator.

Production note:

A 1970's era conference phone sits on the conference table in Scene 1. It looks like a bulked-up table phone. It is a softly rounded, four-sided pyramid that is truncated about three-quarters of the way to the top. On the horizontal surface created by the truncation are a few controls. One of the phone's sloping sides has a rotary dial. On each of the other three sloping sides is a grill through which sound passes. Two traditional desk phones are used in Scene 2.

[Scene 1]

> SANDRA, ARTHUR, and LUCINDA are seated at a small conference table on which rests a conference phone. There may be a small sofa and other items in the room. Everything is tasteful and expensive. The three editors are well-dressed in professorial style. They are all fit and slender. They speak in refined accents. On another side of the stage is an upholstered chair and lamp—older furniture that's part of MARGARET REYNOLDS' home. There is also a small table and a telephone. The NARRATOR addresses the audience and then takes a seat at the conference table to become either SANDRA or LUCINDA.

NARRATOR: It is 1975. Sandra McKnight, Arthur Warrington, and Lucinda Brodeur are editors at the University of Minnesota Press. Their job is to meticulously edit manuscripts that become the Press's scholarly books. They are waiting for a phone call from the Head Editor, Margaret Reynolds. Margaret is dying of cancer and has been working from home.

ARTHUR: Do you think she'll be back?

SANDRA: I can't imagine. If she's working from home, she's obviously in a bad way, and no one says her cancer is going to get any better.

LUCINDA: Yes, I think we're talking about months here. As far as actual work, maybe just weeks. Or, maybe it's the end right now. Maybe that's what this call will be about.

> MARGARET REYNOLDS, obviously very ill, enters and seats herself in her chair. Exhausted from the effort, she pulls a blanket over herself.

SANDRA: One of us is going to become the new head editor.

ARTHUR: Yes, Margaret has been here more years than the three of us together, but Ian will definitely appoint one of us.

SANDRA: Seems to me we're all pretty much equal in qualifications.

ARTHUR: It will be awkward. Whomever Ian appoints, the other two are going to ask "Why wasn't it me?"

SANDRA: I wonder if Margaret will finish the Saunders manuscript. I can't imagine a healthy person surviving that nightmare—let alone someone who is dying. (*Looks at her watch.*) She should have called by now.

ARTHUR: No one but Margaret would have even *considered* editing the Saunders manuscript with advanced cancer. *(With sardonic laughter.)* If I become Head Editor, one of the biggest perks of the job will be making sure it will be one of you who gets manuscripts like that one.

SANDRA: Yes, but that's Margaret. She took it on because it *was* such a mess.

Gathering strength, MARGARET slowly dials.

LUCINDA: *Wild Birds of Minnesota* is a very promising title for us. It will sell. But what misery! The writing is garbled. Half the facts are wrong. The captions don't correspond to the photographs. What was Ian thinking?

SANDRA: I know perfectly well what he was thinking. That baby will be pure profit. Not only will it sell, but the manuscript came with grant money from the State. Enough money to cover editorial, production, and printing costs.

ARTHUR: That's probably why Saunders left it such a mess. He wouldn't have dared to submit a manuscript like that if he weren't absolutely certain we'd take it.

The conference phone rings. ARTHUR stands and leans toward the phone, making clear that he will be the one speaking with Margaret.

ARTHUR: Hello. Hello, Margaret. Thank you for calling. I'm hoping you're feeling OK. The three of us are here. We've all been thinking about you.

MARGARET: Thank you, Arthur. My thanks to you all . . . This is going to be brief. I can't go on any longer. I'm going to resign today. I've already spoken several times to Ian, so today will just make it official. A companion has moved in with me. She's very nice. She'll take good care of me. If I can, I'll die right here at home.

ARTHUR: We are so sorry. You trained all of us. You've taught us so much. You've managed the editorial side of the Press so well and for so long. It's hard to even think about this place without you.

MARGARET: That's just what you have to do. Ian is deciding who will become Head Editor, but he hasn't said much about it to me.

ARTHUR: None of us has been thinking about who the next head editor might be.

MARGARET'S face shows skepticism.

MARGARET: One more thing. I'm handing back the Saunders manuscript. I tried, I really tried, but I barely got a start on it. As you know, it's in very bad shape. I wanted to free up the rest of you for other titles. But, it's not going to work out that way. I'm afraid we'll be—you'll be—under a lot of pressure to make our deadlines for the Fall releases. I'm sorry.

There is perceptible disappointment in the room.

ARTHUR: Margaret, you should just think about your . . . health. We can handle the Saunders manuscript.

There is another visible pulse of disappointment at the phrase "Saunders manuscript."

MARGARET: Well, that's it. I'll try to call in now and then. Just to see how you are all doing. The Press has been my life, and it's been a rewarding life. You folks have been a big part of that. Thank you.

ARTHUR: Thank you, Margaret. For everything.

MARGARET: Good-bye, Arthur.

ARTHUR: Good-bye.

They hang up.

ARTHUR: Well, I guess you heard. That's it.

LUCINDA: That was . . . so sad.

SANDRA: Well, looks like we have *Wild Birds of Minnesota* to edit.

ARTHUR: What are we going to do? Ian may not appoint the new head editor for weeks. One of us is going to have to take it on, and we need to decide now who that will be.

SANDRA: I have a thought about this.

ARTHUR: What?

SANDRA: Jean Farber. She's been wanting to move from Production to Editorial for a year or more. She asked Ian several times. She asked

Margaret. Margaret was open to it, but Ian kept delaying. Well, let's give Jean her big chance: *Wild Birds of Minnesota*. Sink or swim!

ARTHUR: We're just setting her up to fail.

SANDRA: She's a damn good proofreader. She *says* she can edit Press books. This is the moment. We can tell Ian that Margaret recommends Jean for the Saunders manuscript. That will suffice for him. If it's a disaster, none of us are responsible. It will just prove what we always say: Nobody can be a university press editor without a master's degree.

[Scene 2]

> JEAN is sitting at her desk, editing a very thick typescript with a blue pencil. The desk and her chair are utilitarian at best. The audience can see the many hand-written annotations on the page she is holding. Her workspace is neat, but there are stacked reference books and lots of file folders as well as a coffee mug and desk telephone. JEAN is less well dressed and less refined in her speech than SANDRA, LUCINDA, and ARTHUR. The part of the set representing MARGARET'S home remains on stage. MARGARET enters slowly and painfully and dials a call. JEAN'S phone rings, and she answers.

JEAN: Hello.

MARGARET: *(In a severely strained voice.)* Hello, Jean. This is Margaret Reynolds.

> JEAN is taken aback, both by the caller and her voice.

JEAN: Yes . . . Yes . . . Miss Reynolds.

MARGARET: Jean. I wanted to check in with you. I was talking to Ian, and he said that you're editing the Saunders manuscript. Is that correct?

JEAN: Yes . . . Miss Reynolds.

MARGARET: You can just call me "Margaret."

JEAN: Yes, Margaret.

MARGARET: So, how is it going?

JEAN: I think it's going well. There's a lot of work to do. I'm lucky. My husband is pretty much taking care of the baby, or I couldn't do this at all. Margaret . . . the manuscript really is a disaster. Not only is the writing unclear, but when I query Professor Saunders, he's evasive. I think he's lost his notes, and often he *can't* answer my queries. I've done some searching in the library, and I've phoned other ornithologists. But . . . Margaret . . . I like the work. I wish I had more time, but I *can* get this manuscript to Press standards. I will do it. You know how I've been asking to move from proofreading to editing. Well, this is my big chance, and there's nothing I won't do, nothing that will stop me.

MARGARET: What's the deadline, Jean?

JEAN: May 1 for the text, and May 9 for the index.

MARGARET: May 1! An index! This is very unfair, Jean. *My* deadline was May 1. I'm very surprised that they didn't set the deadline back. And how could they not have hired an outside indexer? Do you even know how to index?

JEAN: Well, I've read Hargrove, and I've studied the indexes of some Press books. I can compile the index.

MARGARET: Who have you been working with on the Editorial side? Who gave you the May 1 deadline? Who assigned you the index?

JEAN: Sandra.

MARGARET: Sandra. Hmm . . . Jean, I wish there were something I could do about this. Unfortunately, I'm retired now.

JEAN: *(Clearly upset.)* I wish you were still in the building with us.

MARGARET: Yes. I would have loved to have worked with you. Helped you grow into a Press editor. Now you're going to have to do that on your own.

JEAN: Yes. But I can. This is the work I was born to do. Just like you, Margaret.

MARGARET: Indeed, just like me . . . I need to get off the phone now. I think this will be our last conversation. I'm glad we had it. If I'd been at work, all this would have been handled differently. I'm sorry, but that just wasn't in the cards. Good-bye, Jean.

JEAN: *(Struggling to hold back tears.)* Good-bye, Margaret.

[Scene 3]

> MARGARET, looking healthy, stands at the gates of Heaven facing ST. PETER. ST. PETER has a welcoming manner. Meanwhile, JEAN continues to work quietly at her desk.

ST. PETER: Margaret Reynolds. There wasn't the slightest question regarding your admission to Heaven. You have lived a blameless life—no vices, no bad behavior, just hard work, and kindness and consideration for everyone around you.

MARGARET: Thank you. My life consisted very largely of my work as an editor of scholarly books. Some were important, many were less so. But editing these books was my way of contributing to the world's knowledge, the deeper understanding of everything around us.

ST. PETER: Margaret Reynolds. You realize there will be no editing in Heaven. There is no editing of manuscripts because there is no imperfection. We have no police, no military, no surgery.

MARGARET: Oh my. It never occurred to me that I'd need to find something else to do with my time.

ST. PETER: Margaret, you never married, always lived alone. You had few friendships. You didn't travel or even take vacations. I believe that more is due to you—especially since you will not be able to continue with the work to which you gave your life. Is there perhaps some way in which I can reward you for your blameless life?

MARGARET: I was never unhappy. There's nothing I would ask for. But . . . perhaps, perhaps there is. Perhaps the skills that I developed over a lifetime of exacting editing—the ability to find just the right word, to fix a disorganized page simply by moving one sentence and one clause, the discipline to keep 500 facts clear in my mind, my way of working tactfully with authors to guide them in the right direction. If it were possible, I'd bestow this gift upon someone, a young editor of my acquaintance.

ST. PETER: I know of whom you speak. Tell me more.

> JEAN sets down her red pencil. She's imbued by an unearthly influence. She stands.

MARGARET: Even now she shows talent, and she fully shares my passion, my dedication. She has a loving husband and a young child. I'm very glad about that.

> JEAN understands what is happening. She slowly turns her head toward MARGARET and ST. PETER.

MARGARET: So, my request is that we merge my talent with hers. And, if it is possible, give her some inkling, some intuition, that this is *my* gift, that, in a sense, she is my daughter in the discipline of scholarly editing.

ST. PETER: *(Turning toward JEAN.)* It is done.

> A powerful wave passes through JEAN. She has been transformed.

MARGARET: And one more thing. I ask that if Jean proves worthy, and I know she will, I ask that when her time comes, when she leaves this world, she too will be able to bequeath her gift to another dedicated young editor. She will want to do that.

ST. PETER: This too is done. Follow me, please, Margaret Reynolds.

> JEAN watches them leave, sits, pauses to think deeply, and returns to her editing.

The End

Postscript to "Margaret Reynolds Enters Heaven"

This play is set in a corner of the academic world, the university press. The proper role of a university press is the dissemination of knowledge with the least possible regard for revenue. But we learn that commercial thinking has deeply pervaded this university press. In contrast, Margaret has devoted her life to her craft and the ideals of scholarly publishing. So while this is very personal story, we see in the background the contrast between the knowledge-driven and the corporate university in the arena of scholarly publishing.

The first two scenes follow actual events. But the idea underlying Scene 3—that the actual "Margaret Reynolds," as she left this world, gave a special gift to my wife, Jean Farkas—was not something I invented for this play. I am no believer in the supernatural, but a half-belief that Jean received this gift has lived inside me for decades.

Forgiveness

A 10-Minute play by

David K. Farkas

Characters:

Sam Dowling: An older man, head of an academic department in the engineering college of a major university. He is dying of a brain tumor.

John Dowling: Sam's deceased son, in his 30s, who appears in apparitional form. He is dressed in untidy worker's clothing that is bleached nearly white to suggest that he is an apparition. His walk is not quite human. Colored stage lighting may be used.

Tim Ellison: An assistant professor, recently mentored by Sam.

Sharon: An associate professor, once mentored by Sam.

Physical Therapist

Bess Dowling: Sam's deceased wife, who appears in apparitional form. She too is dressed to suggest an apparition.

Suggested minimum casting:

Tim

Sam Dowling

Sharon/Bess Dowling (Requires a quick costume change in Scene 4.)

Physical Therapist/John Dowling

[Scene 1]

 TIM and SHARON are standing and talking.

TIM: I'm going to visit Sam this afternoon. He's done so much for me. And he accomplished so much . . . for the Department, for the whole discipline.

SHARON: But there was a big price to pay.

TIM: Yes, I never knew of anyone who had two family members commit suicide. That's so terrible. It's crazy.

SHARON: Not so crazy. When John did it, Bess couldn't stand the pain. Nothing's worse than your child shooting himself.

TIM: Just think of it. Sam just going and going, year after year with all that tragedy behind him.

SHARON: Yes, he lived for his work.

TIM: But it's tough to be dying with no family around you and such awful things to remember. I guess he can look back on all he accomplished during his career. I hope that's enough.

SHARON: This whole thing is so sad.

SHARON and TIM embrace lightly. They exit.

[Scene 2]

TIM has come to visit SAM in a nursing facility's physical therapy room. SAM is wearing hospital pajamas and has a bandage wrapped around his head. There is a walker near him. On the floor is a child's ring-sorting toy with its post partially filled with a few brightly colored rings. The PHYSICAL THERAPIST is holding one of the rings in his hand.

PHYSICAL THERAPIST: Come in. You must be visiting Sam. You're very welcome to join us.

TIM approaches.

PHYSICAL THERAPIST: Sam, why don't you show your friend how well we're doing? Now reach down—slowly now—and get the blue ring.

SAM: *We're* not doing anything. And I'm sick of your damn rings. Pick it up yourself.

PHYSICAL THERAPIST: Sam, we're not going to make much progress if we don't work on the ring exercise. I know you want to retain your mobility.

SAM: I'm mobile enough. *(Kicks the rings and the spindle with its base across the room.)* How's that for mobility? I'm done with this.

The PHYSICAL THERAPIST reacts in surprise. SAM does an aimless circuit around the stage, looking at nobody. He exits, walking stiffly.

TIM: This man is chair of an engineering department at the University. He's the head of Northwest Search and Rescue. Why do you think he's going to play with children's toys? Can't you at least get an adult-looking version of that thing?

PHYSICAL THERAPIST: *(Stiffly)*. I don't purchase the equipment.

[Scene 3]

TIM and SHARON are standing and talking.

SHARON: It's just a matter of weeks, maybe not even that.

TIM: I'm going to see him tomorrow morning.

SHARON: Sometimes his head is clear, sometimes it's not. But mornings are better. I visited yesterday. He hardly said anything, but he knew that I was there.

TIM: I'll see how it goes.

[Scene 4]

SAM is in a wheelchair staring blankly into space. There's a bandage around his head. TIM enters. After a few moments, SAM notices TIM, but doesn't recognize him. Throughout the scene, SAM speaks slowly, his energy is limited.

SAM: *(Mind wandering.)* You're from the Dean's office. You're the new outreach coordinator.

TIM reacts in surprise and pain.

TIM: No, I'm Tim.

SAM: Welcome aboard. You'll like working for the College . . .

TIM: Tim. Tim Ellison.

SAM: . . . I've been here 38 years, and I'm still going strong. This place just keeps me invigorated . . .

TIM decides to play along.

TIM: Thank you, Professor Dowling.

SAM: Your name is?

TIM continues to play along.

TIM: Thank you. I'm . . . Bob Wilson. Dean Bishara asked me to talk to you about the College's new industry partnership initiative.

SAM: *(Gathering energy.)* Now, about the industry partnership initiative . . . I'm confident that you'll find that this department is very well prepared to participate. We already have an industry advisory board that meets . . .

JOHN enters in apparitional form. He is a projection of SAM'S imagination. He carries an open, half-empty bottle of whisky. The bulge in his pocket turns out to be a pistol. TIM takes no notice of JOHN. The play has become surreal. The audience is now seeing the action as filtered through SAM's mind. SAM is dismayed and distracted by JOHN'S aggressive manner.

SAM: . . . that meets . . . twice a year. Boeing, Microsoft . . . Amazon—all represented. *(Faltering.)* About ten . . . more tech companies. Also . . . the major public utilities—Seattle City Light, Puget . . . Power.

JOHN: *(Gruffly and with sardonic, slightly threatening humor.)* Bob, you forgot to introduce me. I'm the other outreach coordinator. I'm John. John . . . Dowling . . . your . . . assistant.

What takes place on stage is primarily SAM'S imagination and does not always make sense. TIM sees JOHN, addresses him as a colleague, but also identifies him as SAM'S son.

TIM: Oh, that's right. I'm sorry. Professor Dowling, this is John Dowling. He's your son.

JOHN: That's right. You remember me, Dad. Don't you?

SAM: *(Focuses his attention desperately on TIM.)* We have a database of department alumni—probably more complete . . . than the one in the Dean's Office.

JOHN: Fuck your database, Dad. What do you think Mom thinks of your database? Shall I ask Mom to join the party?

As if on cue, BESS enters in apparitional form and stands impassive at the periphery.

JOHN: Hey, Dad. Is she going to be your wife? Or is she going to be some flunky from the Dean's office? This is your fantasy, so you get to choose.

SAM hesitates and then sputters.

SAM: Ah . . .

JOHN: *(In a taunting tone.)* Can't make up your mind—huh?

SAM: Ah . . .

JOHN: Hey, Bob—would you like another "assistant"? Here she is.

JOHN points to BESS. BESS steps forward.

TIM: *(To JOHN.)* Stop!

TIM'S next speech is partly TIM'S actual speech as he tries to draw SAM out of his disturbing reverie and partly what SAM makes up in his own mind as he tries to return to his wish-fulfillment fantasy about the visit from Bob Wilson.

TIM: Sam, listen to me! . . . Let's get back to business. I'm Bob Wilson, the . . . new outreach coordinator. Dean Bishara asked me to talk to you about the College's new industry partnership initiative.

JOHN: Fuck your dean. Fuck your database. Think about your life, Dad. Think about your wife—for once. Think about me—for once. You ignored us when we were alive. Now you're trying to forget all that in your last moments. Sorry, it doesn't work like that.

TIM: *(To JOHN.)* For God's sake . . . Why do you need to torture the man?

JOHN takes a swig from the bottle.

JOHN: Shut up. Stay out of our business.

SAM: I loved Bess. I did. When we traveled, some guys found women. I never did.

JOHN: Sorry, that's not enough. Your brand of unfaithfulness was worse. It went on decade by decade.

BESS: *(To JOHN.)* He cared about us both. He was just . . . busy . . . preoccupied.

JOHN: He was always disappointed in me. Ashamed. Tell me I'm wrong, Dad. Tell me. Am I wrong?

SAM: OK. Say it. Say it all. I deserve it. But, in my worst moments, burying you, burying Bess, I never thought about putting a gun to my mouth like you did. For all my faults, I had beliefs, values, the strength to persevere. You had nothing, no strength of any kind. You didn't try to do *anything* with your life.

JOHN: That's right. Let it all come out. Well, you know what? The way my life turned out—that's on you as much as me.

TIM: *(To JOHN.)* Stop torturing the man!

SAM: Tim, I'm torturing *myself*. I know what's happening. I *brought* John and Bess here. John is right. I have no business trying to dodge all that I did . . . What I did, and what I didn't do. What I did wrong—very wrong.

JOHN: That's right, Dad. I'm here to *enjoy* your suffering. *(Drinks from the bottle.)* Let's call it a little "family time."

BESS: John, what are you doing this for? Does it do any good? I've forgiven Sam. Why can't you?

JOHN: Why should I forgive him? Why did *you*? He doesn't deserve forgiveness.

SAM: I don't. I know that.

> BESS takes JOHN'S arm and walks him away from SAM and TIM. SAM finally recognizes TIM and regains control of himself.

SAM: Hello, Tim. Thanks for stopping by. It's really nice to see you. Tim, are you married? I'm having trouble remembering.

TIM: Yes, Sam. My wife is Susan. You've met her.

SAM: That's right. Of course. Very nice young woman . . . Tim, it's important to have a rewarding career. It's good to work hard at it. But not the way I did. Do you understand?

TIM: Yes. Thank you. I'll remember.

BESS: *(Addressing JOHN.)* Forgiveness is not about whether it's deserved. The whole point of forgiveness is that it's *not* deserved. This is the one thing you can still do, John. So do it. You don't have to *love* your father. But you can *forgive* him.

JOHN: No.

BESS: Forgive him for my sake. You always loved me, and I loved you more than anything else in the world. Walk right over to your father and tell him you can forgive him.

SAM: Remember what I'm saying, Tim. Don't neglect your family.

JOHN: I can't forgive him. Perhaps I should. But I can't. That's one of the differences between you and me.

BESS: Try.

JOHN pauses, conflicting emotions running through him.

JOHN: I'll do what I can.

JOHN walks over to SAM.

JOHN: Dad, you can call this forgiveness if you want to. I can at least end your misery. *(Pointing his gun at SAM.)* Here is my gift to you.

SAM looks straight up at JOHN and at the barrel of his gun.

SAM: Thank you, son.

JOHN shoots SAM at close range, but no shot is heard. SAM's chest spasms and his head shakes. He slumps over in his wheelchair. He has died a natural death. BESS takes JOHN's hand affectionately and leads him offstage. TIM returns to SAM.

TIM: Sam. Sam? God!

TIM briefly examines SAM. Then TIM walks hurriedly to the far side of the stage and, as though it were a corridor, calls loudly.

TIM: We need someone here! Quick! We need someone.

TIM: *(Thinking out loud.)* No one knows the future. But I'm not going to die like Sam. That much I can make happen.

SHARON enters and joins TIM. (We've jumped forward in time.)

SHARON: You were there when he died?

TIM: Yes, when I came in, Sam was alert. We talked. Then . . . things happened. He was talking, but not exactly to me. He was very . . . emotional, very upset. Then, he just faded out and died. I got a nurse, but it was over.

SHARON: Perhaps just as well . . . When you talked, what were you talking about?

TIM: At first it was OK. He imagined that I was someone from the dean's office. I was fine with that. But then he sort of got crazy. He talked personal stuff. Things about his life that he regretted. Bess. His son. It was all sort of garbled, but he was full of guilt and sorrow.

SHARON: My God! Tell me more about what happened.

TIM: I'm sorry, but I don't want to repeat any of it. At least not yet.

SHARON: I understand.

TIM: No one will ever know what his final moments were like, what he was thinking. But I think that maybe, just maybe, at the moment of his death Sam found forgiveness.

The End

Postscript to "Forgiveness"

The core of this psychological tragedy is the complex final scene in which the actual circumstances of Tim Ellison's visit with Sam Dowling are blended with Sam's two warring fantasies. Sam tries to re-live his successful professional life by imagining that Tim is a young staff member from the dean's office. However, Sam's grievously failed personal life asserts itself as well. As Sam dies from his brain tumor, he imagines that he has been shot by his son, but that the shooting is at least a partial act of forgiveness.

Navigation Problem

A 10-minute play by

David K. Farkas

Characters:

Don: He is in his late 20s or early 30s, handsome and athletic. He is dressed for an academic conference but is disheveled and drunk.

Lisa: She is in her late 20s or early 30s, attractive, and dressed for an academic conference.

DON, obviously intoxicated, makes his way along the downtown street. He is clearly having trouble finding his destination. He exudes misery.

LISA: Hey there. Looks like you're having a navigation problem. Would you like a bit of help?

DON: I'm alright.

LISA: You're here for the MLA conference—yes?

DON: That's right.

LISA: Which hotel are you staying at?

DON: The Jackson.

LISA: Well, then you're headed in the wrong direction.

DON looks around confusedly.

LISA: It's this way. I can walk you there.

DON: No need.

LISA: Maybe yes. Maybe no. Anyway, it's just three blocks. It's a nice enough evening, and I don't mind a bit of a stroll.

DON looks at LISA and likes what he sees.

DON: OK, then. Thanks.

They begin walking, slowly and with occasional pauses. They walk side by side but not far from each other because they are presumably on a sidewalk.

LISA: I'm guessing that you're faculty.

DON: No, I'm not faculty.

LISA: Hmm. A graduate student, then. We turn here. *(Guides him.)*

DON: No, I'm not affiliated with any academic institution.

LISA: You're with a publisher. Maybe textbooks.

DON: No, not that either.

LISA: Then you're a private scholar! So am I. Not many of us here.

DON: Not that either.

LISA: Some wealthy professor brought their personal trainer to the conference? You do look very fit.

DON: No. But thanks for the compliment.

LISA: Then you're a total mystery man. *(She guides him to turn a corner.)* This way. I'm your new friend, so tell me, Mystery Man, what do you do and why are you attending an MLA conference?

DON: *(With an air of reckless bravado.)* I'm . . . an academic pirate, an academic prostitute.

LISA: Well, "prostitute" is a misdemeanor. "Pirate" can get you into real trouble. What kind of piratical prostitution do you do?

DON: Nothing I need to talk about. Nothing you'd want to hear.

LISA: Well, I'd be the expert on what I want to hear. I can stop you easily enough.

DON: Why do you want to know anything about me?

LISA: Just interested. You're a mystery man. Definitely more interesting than the typical assistant professor. Are you ashamed that you're an "academic prostitute"? I don't have any prejudice against that line of work.

DON: No, I'm not ashamed. My attitude is defiance, not shame.

LISA: Defiance. Whoa! Now you *got* to tell me. What's your story, Bluebeard? *(Teasing.)* I got a story of my own. You show me yours, and I'll show you mine.

> DON laughs. He is intrigued by LISA'S wit as well as her appearance.

LISA: Here we are, the Jackson.

> They step through an imaginary doorway and into the lobby of a large hotel. A sofa and potted plant are carried on stage, perhaps with other items that suggest the lobby of a hotel.

DON: Thank you. Want to sit in the lobby?

LISA: Yes, but let's stay away from the area where the cocktail waitresses come to take drink orders. You've had enough for tonight, and I'm not much for alcohol.

DON: *(Gestures.)* How about right here?

LISA: Sure.

> They sit on the sofa.

LISA: So why are you at the conference?

DON: Looking for business—clients . . .

> DON looks off in the distance to where the lobby melds into the cocktail lounge.

DON: Let me go over there and ask the waitress to come over here. I'll do a round of drinks. She sure isn't getting much business tonight.

LISA: Not a lot of drinking at an MLA conference.

DON: Yep. She'd be a lot busier if this were a conference for auto parts dealers or pediatricians. I'll go get her.

LISA: No, don't . . . You said, "You're looking for business"?

DON: That's right. I'm an enemy of the academic system. A privateer. I was one of *the* best English graduate students at Iowa State. I wrote a first-rate dissertation. But when I finished, there were like zero—well, almost zero—jobs in 19th century literature. I published an article from my dissertation. I gave a presentation at a regional conference. That wasn't enough. The English Department let me keep my teaching assistantship for another year. I published *another* article. Gave *another* presentation. But no job—not even at some little podunk college. Then the English department was done with me. I was shop-worn goods, just an academic hanger-on. I'd followed the rules, done everything you were supposed to do to join the professoriate. But the system wasn't giving me what I'd worked for, dreamed of. So, fuck the system. Now I write dissertations—well, usually the graduate student has most of a dissertation written, but it's a mess. I write journal articles—well, I start with whatever my client has written and do something with it. I'm strong in theory, so I can find an angle on almost any author.

LISA: Students get term papers written for them on the internet. Or, they just buy a ready-to-go term paper on a topic that fits their assignment. Now it's AI.

DON: Yeah. But I work with faculty and graduate students. I get 5K for one of my projects. These topics are way too specialized for generative AI. If someone is approaching their tenure decision, what I offer is damn well worth 5K.

LISA: How do you find clients at MLA?

DON: Mostly I attend the professional development sessions—"How to Finish Your Dissertation," "Overcoming Writer's Block," "Getting Your First Article Accepted for Publication." I have an eye for the people who look desperate. I chat with these folks and take a good close look at their name tags. Then, a few weeks later, those folks get an email— "Hushmail," "Tessian," totally untraceable. Usually, they don't even know I saw them at the conference. But I demonstrate my credentials, make a deal, and get paid through Venmo in a special account. If they get caught somehow, I'm in the clear.

LISA: Well, you *are* a pirate, then. I'll leave it to you whether you're a prostitute or not. You're no sex worker, but I guess you've prostituted your talents.

DON: And you? You said you're a private scholar—you just come here for fun? For ed-i-fi-cay-shun?

LISA: That's right. This is just a treat I give myself every year. I go to lots of sessions. I like to ask questions during the Q/A. Actually, I publish pretty regularly. Feminist theory and neocolonialism. Nothing earth-shattering, but journals take my stuff. I enjoy academia, even though I don't teach. And I like talking with professors. That's one reason why I was looking to chat with you—although this here isn't the kind of academic conversation I was expecting.

DON: Are you a lawyer or something that you can afford to do this?

LISA: No. Not a lawyer. Actually, I'm not so different from you—you said "prostitute." Well, I'm exactly that—an academic sex worker.

DON: *"Academic* sex worker"?! That is totally crazy. What do you mean?

LISA: All my clients are professors. I live in Boston, and there are a hell of a lot of professors in Boston and Cambridge. Like everyone else, professors have sex drives and maybe fantasies they can't fulfill at home. But they are petrified at the thought of low-life girls. Girls who might have diseases. Maybe work with criminals who might blackmail them. Who knows what. But these guys feel safe and comfortable with me. And we have great literary conversations.

DON: How did all this happen?

LISA: You were screwed by the system? I think I got more screwed than you. I always loved literature. Went straight from college to graduate school—Northeastern. It was everything I wanted. Then, in my third year, one of my favorite professors—Ed Ryan—offered me a fellowship to be his research assistant in England over the summer. I'd never been to Europe. Working closely with Ed all summer seemed perfect. I'd been planning to find a dissertation topic that he could direct. So this was the greatest thing that could happen to me.

DON: But he required sex?

LISA: No, he was smarter than that. The way he presented it, everything was on the up and up. Separate accommodations. Never mentioned sex at all. But he was betting . . . he knew how it would go. And, pretty soon, we were making love. And I was fine with that. Added romantic flair to the summer. I didn't really think I was doing anything wrong—not in a big way at least. Eight years ago, there was nothing so unusual about a female graduate student having an affair with her professor. Everyone's more careful now.

DON: So what happened?

LISA: His wife found out. Divorced him. Made an enormous stink and divorced him. Turned out my "fellowship" was his household money. He had opened a bank account in the name of some bogus scholarly foundation, and that's where my stipend checks came from. I had no idea. Never thought twice about it. But when the big blow-up came, absolutely no one saw things my way. I was a slut, a prostitute, taking the man's money for sex—and to get ahead of the other graduate students. Northeastern started an investigation, designed to take forever. Meanwhile, I couldn't even register for courses. And I was notorious—no other graduate school—anywhere—would take me.

DON: I'm sorry.

LISA: But I got subtle inquiries from faculty—first Northeastern, but then other local schools. These men told me that they were very sympathetic with my situation. It was totally unfair that I'd lost my teaching assistantship. They were ready to help me financially, but this time sex was definitely part of the deal.

DON: So you got screwed by the academic system, just like I did. And now you do your own screwing! Are you recruiting here?

LISA: Ha. No, not at all. *You* have an internet business. My business is "face to face"—brick and mortar, as they say. But I don't run out of clients back in Boston. Men aren't much inclined to tell other men about women they are paying for. But, on occasion, I ask a client—as a special favor—to help me identify prospects. And they do.

DON: You said married men.

LISA: Yes, unfortunately most are. That's the bad part. But ducking out on their wives is their problem, not mine. And I don't keep much in the way of written records or a client list. If my relationship with a client is exposed—and it hasn't happened yet—that wouldn't actually affect the rest of my business.

DON: So, we're both pirates. Kicked out of the academic system, and now we live off that system.

LISA: Something like that. But you know, Don, there are some big differences between us. You deal in dishonesty, deceit. I bet that through most of your academic career you despised plagiarism. Now that's who you are. And I don't think you're exactly thriving on it. You sound bitter, lost. I'm not bitter. I make very good money. Have mostly good sex with people I genuinely like. You won't see me staggering around drunk needing help to get back to my hotel. Maybe you need to find a new path in your life. May I ask whether you prefer men or women—or both?

DON: I'm entirely heterosexual.

LISA: OK. That will work. What do you know about sex work, Don?

DON: Well . . . ah . . . I've sometimes engaged women for the purpose of . . .

LISA: Well, so you do know something. And, you've already given up the moral high ground regarding sex work. Here's my deal: I can help you find female clients for your services. Only academics. For these women, your Ph.D. is a real plus. They'd be . . . comfortable with you. Some of the women might be a little older than you'd like. Quite a few are socially awkward. That's what kept them from finding men the regular way. But they would all be women you can talk to, relate to. Is there anything keeping you in Ames? This isn't the kind of business you'd ever want to run in a small city where everyone knows each other.

DON: I have absolutely nothing keeping me in Ames. Just lethargy. But I just don't know about this plan . . . Big change to say the least. I like that all the women are Ph.D.s . . . There *are* a lot of men who would think it's just fine to have women pay *them* for sex. Maybe I could get used to this, Lisa, if I moved out to Boston, and we joined forces, so to speak. I could always change my mind and find some other work.

LISA: That's right. And I can change my mind too . . . You know you'll need to cut way down on your alcohol. Also please keep doing whatever it is you do to have that great body.

DON: I'm ready to cut back on the booze. I'm ready for a new life.

LISA: Don, I think we have a plan. And you'll fill a gap in my social life. I have woman friends, and I have clients. But I wouldn't mind having a good friend who's a man.

LISA rises as if to leave. DON rises to join LISA.

DON: What about you and me—as more than friends? When we met, I was sort of drawn to you. I opened up to you real quick about my personal life. Do you think we might, you know, become a couple in Boston?

LISA: Well, first of all, no sex. I get enough of that from my clients. You may very well feel the same way once you get started. I suppose I'll feel differently about that after I retire. You don't do this kind of work forever.

DON: OK. No sex. But it could be very nice if we just set up a household together. You know, Sunday brunch, walks in the park. Visiting museums.

LISA: Maybe . . . But, I want a man who respects himself, who believes in his life. So, here's my second deal: You come join me in Boston. And when you've re-discovered your passion for scholarship, when you've published your first piece of scholarship with your own name on it, then we can think seriously about a live-in relationship.

DON: I'm ready to do it. There's not much I'll be leaving behind in Ames. And I have a few ideas that I'd like to develop into journal articles.

LISA nods approvingly.

DON: Lisa, when we met, you said that you'd help me with my navigation problem. I believe you have done exactly that.

LISA: *(Smiling.)* I'm very happy that I offered to help you. I don't charge for all my services . . . I'm eager to help you start your new life in Boston. I think you're a lost man about to find himself.

They embrace lightly.

The End

Postscript to "Navigation Problem"

"Navigation Problem" is a quirky comedy, a personal story that takes place at the edges—or perhaps in a dark corner—of the academic world. It looks at the ways you can be a prostitute, the ways you can be "screwed" in the academic world, and how you can be lost—and found—on a city street and then in life itself.

Lisa was screwed by the academic world. (I chose Northeastern University at random.) But she proves psychologically healthy and resilient. Don is a very different case. Although he doesn't engage in sex work, he has truly prostituted himself. He is a lost soul. But his "navigation problem" is solved by Lisa. He will even find his way back to scholarship. Ironically, it is when he turns to sex work that he gives up prostitution.

Professor Jim

A 10-Minute play by

David K. Farkas

Characters:

Daniel B. Resnik: An assistant professor.

Jim Hanson: A janitor in the building where Prof. Resnik works. He's in his 40s.

Ruth Resnik: Wife of Prof. Resnik.

Campus Security Chief: Middle aged. Authoritarian and aggressive in manner.

Campus Security Officer: Takes cues from the chief.

Narrator: Professor Resnik as an older man.

Suggested minimum casting:

Narrator/Dan

Jim/Campus Security Chief

Ruth/Campus Security Officer

Set and special stage directions:

This play requires a split set. Dan Resnik's campus office is represented by a desk and chair, and the Resnik kitchen is represented by a table and chairs. In Scene 10, the set for Dan's office is replaced by the set of the entrance to the computer lab. To make this 11-scene play run quickly and smoothly, most of the scenes end with the actors simply withdrawing to the periphery of the stage rather than actually exiting. As the stage directions indicate, actors sometimes exit or withdraw to the periphery in character and sometimes out of character (as an actor).

[Scene 1]

> The NARRATOR addresses the audience. His briefcase is on the floor near him.

NARRATOR: Many years ago, when I was an assistant professor, I often drove back to campus in the evening and worked in my office. All these years later, I still remember Jim. I'd like to know what happened to him.

> He then turns, picks up the briefcase, and becomes DAN the assistant professor. Now, with the stride of a younger man, he opens his office door and steps inside. He is surprised to see JIM wearing a "professorial" sport jacket, possibly with leather patches on the sleeves, over work clothes consisting of jeans and a plain white T-shirt. JIM is leaning back in the office desk chair with his feet on the desk, smiling in a happy reverie. Seeing DAN, JIM snaps into the present moment.

JIM: I'll get out of your way. Be out in a second.

DAN: You're the janitor.

JIM: I'm Jim.

DAN: I'm Dan.

JIM: I know. "Daniel B. Resnik, Assistant Professor." Your name's on the door.

DAN: "Dan" is just fine.

JIM: My shift doesn't start for another hour. But the rules don't say nothing about not being in the building *before* your shift starts. Suraiya works the day shift. She comes in at 7:30.

DAN: You can hang out in my office whenever you want. Any time I'm not using it. Not a problem.

JIM: Thanks, Professor Resnik.

DAN: How about "Dan"?

JIM: OK, Professor Dan.

DAN: OK, Professor Jim.

JIM: I like that. I should have been a professor. Maybe a psychology professor. I'm interested in people. It's nice to sit in this office. And it's not like there's anywhere else I need to be. Just a shitty apartment . . . Well, you must have work to do. I'll get outta here.

> JIM, as actor, stands and withdraws to the periphery of the stage. DAN, as actor, follows him to the periphery.

[Scene 2]

> JIM, dressed in his work clothes, is cleaning a corridor with a mop and a bucket on wheels. DAN approaches JIM, who stops working.

DAN: Hi Professor Jim.

JIM: Hi Professor Dan.

DAN: What's up?

JIM: I've been officially banned from city buses. If I'm found on a City Link bus, I'm subject to arrest.

DAN: I've never heard of that. What did you do?

JIM: There was this guy. A real business shit. He's sitting by the window, but he had his briefcase on the other seat so that no one could sit next to him. Crowded bus. People standing front to back, and he thinks it's gonna be his fuckin' private limo. Well, it wasn't. I made damn sure someone got to sit in that other seat. A Chinese woman.

DAN: Did you hurt him?

JIM: No, I didn't have to. I just scared him. Later, he got up and talked to the driver. I should have gotten off at the next stop. I coulda just left by the back door. But I stayed on the bus, and two transit police got on, and they took down my name.

DAN: How are you going to get to work?

JIM: By City Link bus, just like always. They have no way to enforce their rule. What, all the bus drivers in the city are going to ask thousands of people for IDs, just to catch me?

DAN: I see your point.

> The actors withdraw to the periphery.

[Scene 3]

> Again, JIM, dressed in work clothes, is mopping a corridor. DAN
> enters carrying his briefcase and approaches JIM, who stops
> working. JIM's T-shirt is kept hidden from the audience as much as
> possible.

JIM: Hi Professor Dan.

DAN: Hi Professor Jim. *(Looks closely.)* What's on that T-shirt? That's horrible! You can't wear that. Where did you get it? Who sells a thing like that?

JIM: I made it myself. I'm something of an artist. I silkscreen my own T-shirts. He's pretty much got her clothes off. Looks like they're gonna have some fun. Pretty cool, huh. Would you like one?

DAN: No! It doesn't look like that woman is having any kind of "fun." Looks like her clothes have been torn off. Jim, you've got to deep-six that T-shirt.

JIM: I'm gonna wear what I want. I've already been written up. I may get fired. I'm the best janitor on campus. I work twice as hard as a lot of the dufus janitors they have here. Look at these arms. *(Flexes his biceps.)* And the union won't support me. They're supposed to be on my side.

DAN: I know you work hard. My office is much cleaner since you've been here. The computer lab looks great.

JIM: And the halls. And the bathrooms. You have no idea what goes on in the bathrooms . . . *(Changing the topic.)* Three different women complained about my T-shirt. They say they don't feel safe in the building. Shit on that.

DAN: OK, maybe they're over-reacting. But women could consider that T-shirt scary. It's certainly X-rated. You can't walk around here in that. You can't even wear that thing downtown.

JIM: I have First Amendment rights. This is a free country.

DAN: Not that free, Jim.

> The actors withdraw to the periphery.

[Scene 4]

DAN enters his office and sets down his briefcase. JIM is leaning back in the office desk chair with his feet on the desk. He is perusing some of DAN'S books.

JIM: Is it OK that I was looking at your books?

DAN: Sure, Jim.

JIM: I should have been a professor. It's a good life, isn't it?

DAN: It is.

JIM: I just never fit in at school. I was smart enough, but I could never follow the rules. Even the rules that made sense. When you're a professor, there aren't many rules to follow. I see all you guys. You come to work any time. You leave any time. You go to class, and you say anything you want, and the students write all that shit down. Goddam do what you want.

DAN: Well, Jim, you're right about that, especially once you're tenured. It is a good job for people who don't like to take orders from a boss.

JIM: What's "tenured"?

DAN: It means they can't fire you.

JIM: Damn!

The actor playing DAN withdraws to the periphery. The actor playing JIM exits and quickly smears some black and some dark red stage makeup on his face, indicating bruises.

[Scene 5]

JIM is cleaning a corridor with a mop and a bucket on wheels. DAN approaches JIM, who stops working.

DAN: Jeez, Jim. What happened to you?

JIM: You know all the computer thefts in the building? All over campus really—Macs mostly. The campus police don't do shit, so I've been doing my own detective work. Real quiet. Two nights ago, I found a computer thief in an office upstairs. I grabbed him, pinned him down hard on the floor. I was going to hold him for the police. Not campus police, but city police—real police. But I didn't know he had two buddies with him, and they knocked me around a little.

DAN: Jim, did you report this?

JIM: Nope. It would just get me into more trouble. The University can't protect its computers, but I'm not supposed to fight with anyone.

DAN: Probably not. But, still, you oughta get some kind of credit.

JIM: *(Making a fist.)* I'll tell you one thing. If those guys come back to campus, they'll pick a different building.

The actors withdraw to the periphery.

[Scene 6]

DAN is seated at his kitchen table. RUTH is standing.

RUTH: I'm tired of your stories about Jim the Janitor. He's no Robin Hood. He's no workingman's hero. He's a misfit. He's probably dangerous. And you're gonna get yourself in trouble. Is there one other person in the Department who even knows who he is?

DAN: Well, folks must see him. If you're in the building at night, you definitely see him.

RUTH: With his obscene T-shirt that shows him raping a woman?

DAN: Wait a minute. The man on the T-shirt probably isn't him. And, no one can say for sure that what's on the T-shirt isn't consensual. He said something about them having some fun.

RUTH: You're looking at me, right in the face, and repeating that crap?

DAN: I'm only being fair. I'm only telling you what Jim said to me.

RUTH: You mean what he'd say to a judge, before he got jail time.

DAN: Jim sees all this as his artistic freedom. He wouldn't hurt anyone. If he saw an actual woman being raped—even with a knife—he'd stop it. He's a good person, just ragged around the edges.

RUTH: I know why you like him. He rejects authority, lives by his own rules—bad ones, unfortunately. There's a little of Jim in you. You dodged authority by becoming a professor.

DAN: Maybe so. But Jim needs to have someone on his side, and it looks like I'm it.

RUTH: I totally understand you. In a way, I even like how you're drawn to Jim. But you've totally lost your perspective on this. It won't end well.

DAN and RUTH, as actors exit. RUTH changes costume to become the Campus Security Officer in Scene 8.

[Scene 7]

JIM, without his bruises, is mopping a corridor. DAN approaches him.

JIM: Professor Dan . . .

DAN: What, Jim?

JIM: I don't think you're gonna be seeing me much longer. I'm appealing, but I'm probably going to be fired.

DAN: I'm really sorry, Jim. That's lousy.

JIM: But I'll tell you what's gonna happen to my supervisor if I get fired, I'm going to bring my crossbow to work and put an arrow through his right kneecap.

DAN: You can't do that. You can't say that. You shouldn't be thinking that.

JIM pantomimes bracing the crossbow against the ground and pulling back on the string to engage the trigger mechanism. Then he lifts the imagined bow.

DAN: Jim, please stop.

JIM: Just like . . . so.

JIM points the bow directly at DAN'S right kneecap and pretends to shoot.

DAN: Jim, you're putting me in an awkward position. I'm supposed to report stuff like that. Jim, tell me you were joking. This is nothing but a crazy fantasy.

JIM: No!

DAN and JIM, as actors, exit.

[Scene 8]

Again DAN is seated at his kitchen table, with RUTH standing.

RUTH: You have to report him. What's wrong with you? Why can't you see that?

DAN: He isn't gonna do anything.

RUTH: Are you sure?

DAN: Not quite.

RUTH: You need to report him. Maybe I will.

DAN: No you won't. I'll deny I ever heard him say anything.

RUTH: Daniel, you're crazy. This has gone way too far. What are you thinking?

DAN: He said "kneecap." Very specifically, "through his right kneecap." If he'd said "through his heart," I'd report him. I'd have to. But he just said "kneecap," and he's in enough trouble already.

RUTH: *(Angry.)* That's right. Who cares about a little ol' kneecap, a little ol' knee? Especially when it's not *your* kneecap. What you're doing—*not* doing—is irresponsible, probably criminal.

DAN and RUTH, as actors, exit. The actor playing DAN quickly puts on a golf jacket to suggest that Dan has been outside.

[Scene 9]

Downstage of the split set, DAN, without his briefcase, approaches RUTH. She may be meeting him in the doorway of their house.

RUTH: Campus Security phoned. You need to go to campus . . . immediately. Your building.

DAN: What happened?

RUTH: They wouldn't tell me. They would have told you.

DAN: Oh my God.

RUTH: Go! Go!

DAN exits in a rush. RUTH exits as an actor. DAN'S office is removed and replaced by four electric fans lined up from upstage to downstage.

136

[Scene 10]

> DAN enters and passes through the (imaginary) main door to his building. He walks a bit farther and sees the electric fans. The CAMPUS SECURITY CHIEF and the CAMPUS SECURITY OFFICER are waiting for him.

DAN: What's going on?

SECURITY CHIEF: *(Pointing to the fans.)* Jim Hanson did all this. We sent him home.

DAN: What's "all this"? Why did he do it?

SECURITY CHIEF: The air conditioner in the computer lab failed. He was trying to blow the hot air out here into the hallway.

DAN: *(Reaching down to feel the current of warm air.)* Trying? It seems to be working.

SECURITY OFFICER: What an idiot! He should have just turned off the machines.

DAN: Not so simple. These are Symbolics workstations. A different beast than a Mac or a PC. It's not obvious how to shut them down. Are the machines still running? I'll take care of that.

SECURITY OFFICER: Yeah, they're running.

SECURITY CHIEF: Hanson went through the building grabbing fans anywhere he could find them. Knocked over people's stuff in the process. Then he went into Wilson Hall and ransacked the building for more fans. He's not even supposed to have a key to that building. He had no authorization to do any of this.

DAN: Those workstations run hot as hell. That's a 90,000 BTU unit in the lab. Keeps the machines from roasting themselves. There's an alarm that's supposed to notify you guys if the air conditioner stops running. What happened?

SECURITY CHIEF: The alarm failed. We're investigating.

DAN: Did Jim phone you for help? Why was this Jim's problem? Why weren't you handling it?

SECURITY CHIEF: Yes, we got a call from Hanson. The guy on duty wrote a service order for the morning.

DAN: A service order? For the morning? Every CPU would have been toast. The servers too. Jim *saved* those machines.

SECURITY CHIEF: There's no evidence for that. We say, repairing the air conditioner in the morning would have been perfectly OK.

DAN: That's ridiculous.

SECURITY CHIEF: What's ridiculous is you arguing. Maybe you should be shutting down those machines, Professor. They're your responsibility now.

DAN: Jim saved the lab—something like half a million dollars, and you're denying it. You screwed up on all fronts. He did what needed to be done, and you're going after him!

SECURITY CHIEF: Save your breath, Professor. Hanson is a loose cannon. He's been a loose cannon since he's been here. We've had enough of him. He's gone. Fired.

DAN: "Loose cannon"? From where I sit, he's a hard-working janitor.

SECURITY CHIEF: You don't know. We've had complaints from women who won't come into the building in the evening because they know he's working there. You're not in charge of security, you're not in charge of janitors, and you'd better deal with those machines you say are at risk of melting down.

DAN: *(Half-turning.)* Damn! Damn this place!

The actors exit.

[Scene 11]

> The kitchen table at the home of DAN and RUTH. DAN is seated and despondent. JIM'S sport jacket is on the table. RUTH stands behind DAN. They are dressed a little differently than in the previous scene.

RUTH: What is that?

DAN: I found Jim's sport jacket in my office. And this. *(Reads from a note.)* "Professor Dan, this is for you. Teach a class for me. Your friend, Jim." This is so sad.

RUTH: He doesn't work for the University anymore. How did he get into your office?

DAN: Are you for real? Jim can get into my building, or any other building, if he feels like it.

RUTH: I'm sorry. But you knew this wasn't going to end well.

DAN: He got totally screwed.

RUTH: Maybe, but he was busy screwing himself.

DAN: I'm going to teach a class in this jacket.

RUTH: What? you'll barely get it on your chest. Your arms will stick three inches out of the sleeves. You'll look ridiculous.

DAN: So, one day I'll look ridiculous. I am going to teach a class in this jacket—for my friend, Professor Jim.

RUTH: OK. OK. Put on his damn sport jacket and teach a class. I really don't care. Thank God, he didn't leave you with his obscene T-shirt. You'd wear *that* to class—then what?

> RUTH'S attitude softens. She puts her arm on DAN'S shoulder. Then she picks up the sport jacket and examines it.

RUTH: I understand. Let's try to make this work. I can have a tailor let out the back and try to get some more length in the sleeves. How it fits won't matter much when you tell your class that the sport jacket isn't yours, that you're wearing it in honor of an old friend.

DAN: Yes, that's what I'll do. *(Assuming a lecturer's voice.)* This sport jacket belonged to Professor Jim Hanson. I am wearing it this afternoon in his honor. Professor Hanson served this institution with great dedication. His career was truly a distinguished one.

The End

Postscript to "Professor Jim"

By and large, this collection of plays endorses the independent spirit of those faculty members who insist on their autonomy, resist administrative control, and sometimes break rules. In "Travel Money" we appreciate the creativity of the Seymour investors and are happy to see them succeed. In "Wasserman the Water Man," we are pleased that Dr. Lewis offers surreptitious support to Wasserman. In "Quality Work," Eric

Sloane initially pushes too hard on his individualism, but he's finally willing to compromise. However, Dan Resnik's case is different. While Dan is in many ways an attractive person, his stubborn loyalty to the wayward janitor is reckless and immoral.

As Ruth recognizes, Jim's individualism resonates with Dan:

> **RUTH:** I know why you like him. He rejects authority, lives by his own rules—bad ones, unfortunately. There's a little of Jim in you. You dodged authority by becoming a professor.

But Dan had no right to bet that Jim will not maim or perhaps even kill his supervisor. Dan cannot even recognize his bad judgment. The Security Chief is dishonest. But Dan is also dishonest in refusing to acknowledge that Jim is a "loose cannon"—when Dan knows even better than the Security Chief that Jim is dangerous. However, a beneficent vision governs the play, and Jim does not carry out his threat. Furthermore, Jim is a survivor. He will bounce through his life, holding fast to his fierce individualism.

The Promise

A 10-minute play by

David K. Farkas

Characters:

Carrie Rosner: A young writer who recently dropped out of the MFA program of the Creative Writing Department at Iowa State.

Professor Ben Morgan: A faculty member under whom Carrie studied.

Professor Mark Terry: Another faculty member in the department.

The Head of the Creative Writing Department: Any gender.

EMT-1: Male if doubled by the actor who plays Mark.

EMT-2: Any gender.

Suggested minimum casting:

Carrie Rosner

Professor Ben Morgan

Professor Mark Terry/EMT-1

The Head of the Creative Writing Department/EMT-2.

[Scene 1]

> BEN'S faculty office, with BEN seated. A thick binder is on his desk. CARRIE is sitting in the visitor's chair. She is dressed carelessly and is agitated.

BEN: I don't exactly appreciate your missing two appointments with me. But, enough of that.

> No reaction from CARRIE.

BEN: Your manuscript is terrific. Very moving. Tragic. But funny, too. And the radial structure through which the themes are developed works very well. This is a major achievement. It's commercial too—something we don't often see around here. Your manuscript will get published, and with a top-line publisher behind you, it will get reviewed, recognized. *Returning to Savannah* will sell.

No reaction from CARRIE.

BEN: I have just a few connections in New York. But they're good ones. I can get you a serious reading by two or three acquisitions editors in major publishing houses. That's all you'll need. All you'll need. Years ago, I had dreams like this for my own writing, but . . . Carrie, I'm so proud that you studied under me—that, in some small way, I contributed to your development as a writer of fiction.

CARRIE: I want it destroyed. Every copy. I've destroyed my copy and every draft. I've deleted every file on my computer. The copy I gave you is the last one. I want it back. That's why I'm here.

BEN: Why are you thinking such a thing?

CARRIE: I don't owe you an explanation.

BEN: I don't understand. There's nothing objectionable about the book. You don't reveal any dark secrets about yourself, or anyone.

CARRIE: Give me the manuscript!

BEN: If there's something I missed, you can delete it—change it. Lots of authors have second thoughts about something personal or controversial they've put into a story. So they change it. You can do that.

CARRIE: That's not it at all. I don't want it published—ever. I don't want anything of mine published. I just want to disappear.

CARRIE reaches across the desk.

CARRIE: Give me my manuscript!

BEN puts his hands on the manuscript and slides it close to him.

BEN: Carrie. I'm not going to let you do this.

CARRIE: Give it to me, you fucker. It's mine. My property.

BEN: Actually, it's not. *(Gestures toward the physical manuscript.)* It's *my* property. You gave this to me. It was a gift. Not a loan. You wanted my opinion of your manuscript. You said nothing about me returning it. Anyway, that's the way I'm looking at the situation.

CARRIE: One more person I couldn't trust. One more betrayal!

BEN: No, I'm doing this for you—for when you reconsider this craziness.

CARRIE: Everyone screws me and says it's for my own good. The people who say they care—the people I trust—they're actually the worst—the poison I drink down because it tastes sweet. That's all you are to me, Professor Morgan, just one more sip of sweet poison. Now give me my manuscript.

BEN: Poison? No! And give you the only copy so you can destroy it? No, I can't do that, Carrie. The manuscript is yours. It really is. But I'm keeping it for you. And maybe the law is screwy, but I do own this copy of your manuscript.

CARRIE: OK, maybe you own those sheets of paper. But I own the words. I prohibit you from getting it published, making more copies, or showing it to anyone—to anyone. That's my right as an artist—yes?

BEN: Yes.

CARRIE: Then do you promise? I mean, *promise*. About this, you won't betray me?

BEN: I promise on my belief in honesty and goodness, my commitment to teaching, and my love for art. I promise you I will not show this manuscript to anyone without your permission. But I will keep it, so that if you decide you want it published—and I think you will—there will be a copy.

CARRIE: But if I never ask to have it published or shown to anyone, you won't show it to even one person. That's regardless of anything that happens?

BEN: Yes.

CARRIE begins to get up, but BEN places his hand on her arm.

BEN: Carrie, can we discuss this change in your attitude? You worked hard on *Returning to Savannah*. Maybe you should speak to a counselor, a psychologist. You may still be eligible to have the University cover this. I'm sure the money part can be handled one way or another. Can we think about this together?

CARRIE gets up from her chair.

BEN: Carrie!

CARRIE: Good-bye, Professor Morgan. Remember your promise.

BEN: Carrie!

BEN begins to get up from his chair, but CARRIE bolts out of his office. With a look of dismay, BEN freezes.

[Scene 2]

MARK and BEN are standing downstage in some unspecified location.

MARK: This is so sad, so tragic. But there were signs. Carrie was acting stranger and stranger. Less friendly. Rosalynn asked her about seeing someone. I think Sakina talked to her as well. You know, our students are mostly young people. And, artistic people are . . . you know. Maybe that's part of being an artist. This has happened here in the past. You know that, Ben. Carrie's suicide is a tragedy we'll all just have to accept.

BEN: It's worse than you know—at least for me.

MARK: What do you mean?

BEN: Carrie wrote an extraordinary novel—finished it. I mean extraordinary. I have a copy.

MARK exhibits surprise. Then he shows increasing interest in the novel and gradually succumbs to a self-interested desire to see it published.

MARK: That's a *good* thing. A very good thing. Carrie achieved something important in her life. Hopefully she knew this, even though she chose suicide.

BEN: Well, it's more complicated. I can never show the manuscript to anyone.

MARK: Not show it? What? What do you mean? Of course you can show it to people, get it published too.

BEN: No, Carrie wanted it to disappear—completely, no trace left behind. She deleted every file, destroyed every print copy. She demanded the copy she'd left with me. I refused to return it. In case she changed her mind. But she made me vow not to show it to anyone, and

144

she's not going to change her mind now. What is there for me to do but destroy it? My God! Do you think I'm going to sit and read it myself? Ben Morgan's bedtime reading. A terrific manuscript by a former student who cursed him and shot herself two hours later.

MARK: What a terrible situation! But you just can't destroy the manuscript. And you can't keep it hidden from the world. Your promise doesn't matter now. Carrie's dead. She will never know whether you kept the promise. She doesn't know anything.

BEN: My promise to Carrie matters as much as ever. I think she knew she was going to commit suicide when she came to my office. This was the one thing she asked me for. I need to keep faith with her.

MARK: No. What matters is for the world to see this novel. The novel is what Carrie will leave behind her. She never seemed to have family or much in the way of friends. Do this for Carrie. Do this for the Department. Don't let Carrie be forgotten.

BEN: She *wanted* to be forgotten.

MARK: Don't you see, Ben? When she came into your office, she wasn't in her right mind. The healthy Carrie is asking you to have the novel published. Don't listen to the sick Carrie.

BEN: We can't just decide that someone was mentally ill and then forget what we promised them. We can't even pass judgment on someone's decision to commit suicide.

MARK: Why are we teaching creative writing if not to bring important literature into the world?

BEN: What's literature for if not to make us more honorable and faithful?

MARK: You know the janitor is pretty casual about security. He'd let me into your office. What does the manuscript look like? I'll handle publication. All royalties go to suicide prevention or something like that . . . You don't even need to describe it. I'll find it. You don't need to think about anything. It's all done.

BEN: *(Spoken ironically.)* Thanks for offering to do my dirty work for me. But I forbid you to conspire with the janitor to illegally enter my office and steal my property. There, that should be definite enough!

145

MARK: Ben, let's imagine that Carrie has returned to us.

MARK, with the gesture of an impresario or magician, ushers an apparitional false-CARRIE onto the stage. She is dressed provocatively. She stands beside him but is inert and robotic.

MARK: I think she'd be grateful to you for preserving her manuscript. She'd surely ask you to have her novel published. Imagine her, Ben. Imagine her right here in this room!

With another gesture, MARK brings this false-CARRIE to life, and she approaches BEN. She functions as MARK'S agent in trying to persuade BEN.

CARRIE: Thank you for keeping the last copy of *Returning to Savannah*!

BEN responds with pleasure. He feels vindicated in keeping the manuscript.

CARRIE: I want it published. *Returning to Savannah* is the one thing I can leave behind. The one trace of my life. You said you can get the novel published. Please do it for me, BEN.

BEN responds with delight. MARK is very pleased.

BEN: Yes. Yes, I will.

As BEN responds fervently to CARRIE, MARK'S face shows triumph.

CARRIE: Ben, you've always been more—much more—than a professor to me.

BEN: You've always been special to *me*, more than you know.

False-CARRIE, stepping backward, returns to MARK'S side and again becomes inanimate.

MARK: You imagined her Ben, didn't you? And she was grateful that you didn't destroy her manuscript. We both know what she wants. Now, let me take it from your office. You don't need to do a thing, not a thing.

BEN ponders, then stares at BEN and false-CARRIE.

BEN: *(Turning on MARK.)* Tempter! Betrayer! You're not thinking about Carrie and her legacy. You're thinking about the reputation of the department. *(A deeper suspicion sets in.)* You want to claim credit for mentoring Carrie! Mark, you are thoroughly corrupt.

MARK: And you're a loser, Ben. What have you written in the last 15 years? Your students know you're a fraud. Everyone does. Do you have friends, Ben? Not many. Have there been women in your life? Not that I know of. You are nothing but a lonely, lonely man—and a no-talent fraud. The "crowning achievement" of your career will be destroying a fine novel.

BEN: Whatever I am. Whatever I'm not. You're worse.

MARK: You're a loser, Ben. A fraud. Lonely and pathetic. Carrie despised you.

BEN: No!

MARK: She did! She did!

BEN: No!

> BEN staggers off stage in grief and confusion.

[Scene 3]

> The DEPARTMENT HEAD is addressing the attendees at a joint memorial service for CARRIE and BEN. MARK stands by her side.

DEPARTMENT HEAD: It is so unusual, so shocking, for a community—for this department is a community—to experience two terrible tragedies in such rapid succession. First the passing of Carrie Rosner, our former student and colleague. Now, just five days later, Professor Benjamin Morgan. Because Professor Morgan—Ben—and Carrie were both part of our community, we've decided to celebrate their lives jointly, as one event. *(Pause.)* I know there's been speculation about whether the two deaths, two suicides—I need to say that—coming one after the other, are somehow linked. I've asked Mark Terry, perhaps Ben's closest friend, to say a few words about this.

MARK: I do not see any connection. Carrie took some classes with Ben, but nothing more than that. The two deaths are just one of those inexplicable events. We need to remember that creative people are a little different from everyone else. They . . . We . . . always live a little bit on the edge. That's part of the creative personality. I worked closely with Carrie, and I'm deeply disappointed that the world will not see any more fiction from this remarkable artist. Just before she . . . passed, Carrie entrusted me with her manuscript. Unfortunately, I had no idea what she was planning to do. But I am talking with several publishing houses, and I am confident that her novel—her first and last novel—*Returning to Savannah*—will be published and will receive the attention it deserves.

DEPARTMENT HEAD: Thank you, Mark. And, I'd like to make the first public announcement of the Benjamin P. Morgan-Carrie Rosner Endowment, to which the department and the University have made founding contributions. The endowment will provide funds for writers in our community who are battling severe emotional problems. You will hear more about the endowment in the coming weeks. *(Pause.)* Reverend Jeffries will now close this, our celebration of the lives of Ben Morgan and Carrie Rosner. Thank you all for attending, for showing your respect and love for Ben and Carrie.

[Scene 4]

> EMT-1 and EMT-2 are kneeling and are examining the prone figure of a dying person (largely hidden from the audience) who will be revealed to be BEN. CARRIE and BEN, in apparitional form, enter and stand together in undefined space near the periphery of the stage. They observe the dying Ben Morgan but exhibit no strong reaction. Instead, they are absorbed in their own conversation.

CARRIE: There was always a special connection between us. You know that. I've always been attracted to you. You're older than me. But I've always hoped you'd become my lover.

BEN: I've imagined us together so many times. I think you are the one woman I can have a life with—be happy with. We'll have our own apartment, not fancy, but perfect for us.

CARRIE: We can work on our writing together. No distractions.

BEN: No publishing houses. No scrambling for recognition.

CARRIE: Just our creative work—forever.

EMT-1: There's still a pulse. But just barely. Should we put a tourniquet around that arm?

EMT-2: There's no point to it. There's internal bleeding from everywhere.

BEN: Carrie . . . I must tell you something. I never destroyed my copy of *Returning to Savannah*. I'm sorry. Everything went so fast. I was in my car, and suddenly knew what I needed to do. I pressed hard on the gas pedal, then swerved into the side of an overpass. Mark Terry will figure out a way to get into my office. He'll find the manuscript. He'll get it published.

CARRIE: Don't worry about it, Ben. It doesn't mean anything to me now one way or the other.

EMT-2: He's almost gone. *(Looking down at the figure.)* Goodbye, mister. Sorry we couldn't help you.

BEN: We're going to be honest with each other.

 BEN gives CARRIE an affectionate embrace.

CARRIE: We'll be so happy together.

 After a brief pause, EMT-2 takes the pulse of the newly deceased BEN MORGAN, then looks at their watch.

EMT-2: Time of death 2:37.

The End

Postscript to "The Promise"

Circumstances have put Ben Morgan in an extremely difficult position. Many people would agree that he did the right thing by refusing to publish Carrie's manuscript. Others would not be bound by Carrie's final demand. But we see Mark Terry change from a helpful friend to an unscrupulous and cruel schemer. He foresees that publishing the manuscript will enhance the reputation of his department, and he hopes to claim credit for mentoring Carrie.

When Ben commits suicide, Mark's path forward is even better. He can now claim credit for mentoring Carrie without fear that Ben will contest this. The memorial service shows how well Mark Terry has succeeded. There is something distasteful about the department chair's eagerness to protect their department's reputation and to engage in some fundraising, but we have no reason to think that the chair questions Mark Terry's account of the events.

As the play closes, we see that Ben has long harbored a fantasy in which he and Carrie are lovers who could enjoy an idyllic life together. This fantasy plays through Ben's mind one more time as he dies by the side of the highway.

This play is not entirely fictional (although the reference to Iowa State is simply a convenience). Many years ago, a graduate student gave me the manuscript of an outstanding comic novel, which I refused to return when she announced her intention of destroying all copies. There is no trace of her on the Internet, and I'm not likely to hear from her again. When I die, my heirs will surely discard my many boxes full of old notebooks and file folders thick with sheets of paper. If they happen to recognize this student's manuscript, they must destroy it.

Tenure Denied

A 10-minute play by

David K. Farkas

Characters:

Assistant Professor Nancy Evans: About 35 years old.

Professor and Department Head Richard Johnson: About 45 years old.

Vice Provost Thomas Sherman: About 50 years old, handsome and well dressed.

Suzie Devereux: A staff writer for the *University News.* About 25 years old, well dressed and physically attractive.

Sets:

Professor Johnson's faculty office. Books and academic journals are visible.

Vice Provost Sherman's sumptuous office. It is replete with the amenities of a high-level administrator.

Note: A split set enables characters to move quickly between Johnson's office and Sherman's office.

Note: For Scene 4, a podium, a chair, and a few appropriate props can be placed (and then removed) far downstage.

[Scene 1]

> PROFESSOR NANCY EVANS sits nervously in the visitor's chair in the faculty office of PROFESSOR RICHARD JOHNSON, head of the Department of Therapeutic Genetics at the health science center of a major research university.

EVANS: I'm very concerned, very worried. I wasn't expecting comments like these from the tenure evaluators.

JOHNSON: Yes. I'm surprised as well.

EVANS: *(Reading from a two-page letter.)* "Despite the obvious importance of Professor Evans' research area, the most recent experimental data are not entirely promising."

JOHNSON: Hmmm. I wonder which of the evaluators wrote *that* letter.

EVANS: *(Reading from another two-page letter.)* "I have reservations about the research methodology. I also note that Professor Evans has not listed any new research funding." Dick, I have several proposals pending. You know that.

JOHNSON: *(Without enthusiasm.)* Yes, Nancy. NIH funding is highly competitive, but I think you've submitted strong proposals.

EVANS: My research, this job . . . is my life. I feel like everything in my life is on the line.

JOHNSON: I'm sure it will all work out.

They speak briefly in pantomime and then freeze.

[Scene 2]

PROFESSOR JOHNSON sits nervously in the visitor's chair in the plush office of THOMAS SHERMAN, the university's vice provost for research.

JOHNSON: My department is desperately short of lab space. We need at least one floor in the new building.

SHERMAN: Everyone's short on lab space. You know that.

JOHNSON: But we've gotten *nothing* these last 10 years.

SHERMAN: You know, Dick. These decisions depend in part on the prevailing winds, and your department hasn't produced any really exciting work in a long while.

JOHNSON: Thomas! Our faculty are highly productive. Our research is respected. I can show you tons of citations. We get more than our share of research funding. What do you mean?

SHERMAN: There's a difference between good research and the research that gets everyone's attention—I mean attention across the whole campus and even with the general public. President Barstow pays attention to publicity, and you know that really big decisions about space allocation always wind up on the president's desk. For your department to compete, you need to showcase something big, really big. Something everyone will take an interest in. What about that Evans woman? Alzheimer's—now there's an exciting research area. You want lab space, new hires, do something with people like Evans.

JOHNSON: Actually, Nancy Evans may not be one of our better stories. Her major research grants run out in 14 months, and she hasn't gotten any new money. Her ideas *looked* promising—exciting even—and, of course, it was easy to get start-up funding for Alzheimer's research. But the findings have not been that impressive. Her AAV vectors haven't altered amyloid deposition. And there are questions about the quality of some of the work coming out of her lab. She's not even a sure bet for tenure.

SHERMAN: Is she at her critical year? Can you move the tenure clock back a year or maybe two?

JOHNSON: Yes, we can move her tenure decision back a year—even two if we cite health problems. Nancy would have to agree to that, of course.

SHERMAN: Well, I think that's what you should do. And, Dick, in the meantime, we need to tell a big Alzheimer's story. You need it, and it helps me too. Frame it like this:

SHERMAN alters his voice in a manner that suggests he's talking to someone other than JOHNSON and that he's extolling Evans' research.

SHERMAN: "Assistant Professor Nancy Evans is doing pioneering work. No one expects her to conquer Alzheimer's all by herself. Other universities, other researchers, will, of course, do their share. But Nancy Evans has already moved the ball from the 20-yard line to mid-field, and she's just hitting her stride. She'll produce new breakthroughs soon."

JOHNSON: "Moved the ball to mid-field"? "New breakthroughs soon"? I don't know that I'm comfortable saying all that.

SHERMAN: Look, Southwestern Tech is the big-time. We all do things we're not comfortable with. You want lab space? Well *earn* it. Tell a story that will shift those prevailing winds in your favor. Whatever the weak points in Evans's research program, just work around them.

JOHNSON: What if she doesn't get more funding? What if she doesn't get tenure? What do we do then?

SHERMAN: That's nothing for *us* to worry about. Most people won't notice if she leaves the university. The rest won't much care. It's all about the present moment, Dick. You need to understand that.

JOHNSON: Well, uh. OK. Thanks, Thomas.

SHERMAN: And remember, this isn't just about lab space. It's for Nancy Evans too. Ultimately, we're about people!

JOHNSON: Yes.

SHERMAN: I think you need to start with a feature in *University News*— print and the website. "Young Southwestern Tech professor—*assistant* professor—is on the forefront of Alzheimer's research." They have a staff writer over there. Susan Devereux—something like that. I haven't met her, but I like her feature articles. Full of enthusiasm, full of hype. She can even make the English Department exciting! Why don't you call Devereux and ask her to do a feature on Nancy Evans. Tell her that I'm behind the idea. Dick, we're going to give Therapeutic Genetics a much bigger profile around here. When you get that whole floor of lab space, other departments won't complain. They'll say, "Of course Therapeutic Genetics got it. Look at all they're doing." Nancy Evans is your story. Hell, I'm Vice Provost for Research, so it's my story too. So go out there and tell it!

> SHERMAN signals that the meeting is over. JOHNSON stands to leave.

JOHNSON: OK. Thanks. Thomas, I'm always grateful for your support.

SHERMAN: You bet, Dick.

[Scene 3]

> SUZIE DEVEREUX stands in THOMAS SHERMAN'S office. To convey that she's in a corner office with large glass windows, she gazes up and down out in one direction, then turns 90 degrees and gazes out again.

DEVEREUX: Amazing views. From this window, you overlook the whole campus. *(She turns her body.)* From this one you look straight over downtown.

SHERMAN: Yes, it's a nice office. Would you like coffee? Tea? Even a glass of wine. *(Gestures toward his desk phone.)* My secretary will bring it here in just a moment.

DEVEREUX: Oh, no thank you.

SHERMAN: Suzie, I need a feature article on a young professor in the Department of Therapeutic Genetics. Her name is Nancy Evans. She's doing extraordinary work on Alzheimer's disease. This can be a great story. I'd like her picture right on the cover. Can you do that?

DEVEREUX: Well, I'm just one of the staff writers. Actually, the most junior. But if I tell the managing editor that this idea comes from you, I'm pretty sure we can get exactly what you want. *(Smiling.)* And, no matter what Nancy Evans looks like, we have photographers and make-up people who can make her very attractive.

SHERMAN: Excellent! . . . One thing. Do all this without talking to Richard Johnson, the department chair.

DEVEREUX: Really? I would normally get a quote from the chair. Something about the great work the researcher is doing.

SHERMAN: Well, not in this case. Professor Johnson is, let us say, behind the times. He doesn't really understand how media works these days.

DEVEREUX: OK.

SHERMAN: Actually, I asked *him* to contact you. But nothing happened. So, I'm stepping in.

DEVEREUX: I assume that Nancy Evans will be helpful.

SHERMAN: Oh, yes. I believe she's very eager for recognition.

DEVEREUX: Then that's what she'll get!

SHERMAN: It's great talking with you, Suzie. I have a feeling we'll be working together in the future.

DEVEREUX: Yes, I hope we get to work together closely. Thank you, Dr. Sherman.

SHERMAN: Thank *you*. And just call me "Thomas." No, "Tom."

DEVEREUX: I hope we get to work together closely—Tom.

SHERMAN: You know . . . Suzie, I can make a lot of good things happen for you. But I'd like just a little strategic input with some of those feature stories. Some of the administrators here are not my friends. Or, they're my friends, but they're also competition. There are ways to say good things about someone, like *University News* always does—but not the *best* things. I'll help you get the clout you need so you can choose what stories you want to write, and then I'll tell you how I need them written. Are you ready to really succeed in the modern university?

DEVEREUX: I'm very ready to succeed, and I think I've found a man who's going to make that happen. It is a real thrill to have Vice Provost Thomas L. Sherman as my mentor—and my friend.

> DEVEREUX stands up and turns to leave in a manner that shows her attractive body to advantage. SHERMAN subtly shows appreciation. DEVEREUX exits.

[Scene 4]

> VICE PROVOST SHERMAN, standing behind a podium and facing the audience, is enthusiastically addressing a group of (imagined) alumni donors. NANCY EVANS is seated near the podium. On her lap is a copy of *University News* with her photograph on the cover. SHERMAN holds another copy.

SHERMAN: And now, a special shout-out to one of Southwestern's brightest young stars—Assistant Professor Nancy Evans . . . in the Department of Therapeutic Genetics. You all may have seen the feature on Nancy in the current issue of *University News. (Proudly shows the cover to everyone in the room.)* Nancy is at the forefront of research on Alzheimer's disease. Her publications are read by every researcher in the field. Major pharmaceutical companies are showing interest . . . Let's have some serious applause for Professor Nancy Evans!

> Loud applause. EVANS, intoxicated by the applause, stands and faces the room. She holds the magazine cover in front of her.

[Scene 5]

> PROFESSOR NANCY EVANS sits in RICHARD JOHNSON's office. She is distraught. She is angry. She holds papers and file folders. On the floor beside her is a briefcase.

EVANS: I couldn't believe it. Six to two against me. One abstention.

JOHNSON: We both know there were problems with your letters. There were questions about your research. And you have no new research funding. I just wish your tenure case had been a little stronger.

EVANS: But I'm at the forefront of Alzheimer's research. I'm a rising star.

JOHNSON: *(Hesitantly.)* One could say that.

EVANS: *(Speaking with increasing intensity.)* It's obviously a conspiracy. People want to get rid of me so they can take over my research program. Run my lab. Take credit for everything I've accomplished. That's what's behind this tenure vote. You should have seen it coming. You should have stopped it. You need to do something now.

JOHNSON: No! . . . No . . . Nothing like that!

It's not true, Nancy.

No one is trying to steal your work.

Listen to me. Please.

> From underneath the papers on her lap, EVANS draws a small handgun and sets it down visibly on top of the papers. She grips the handle and lets the barrel point upward.

JOHNSON: Oh! Oh! My God! Nancy! That's completely unnecessary! Put that thing away. Please. We're friends. I'm completely on your side. I'm not saying that there's a conspiracy, but . . . maybe there's been a bad tenure decision. I understand that you've been under tremendous stress. So, put that gun away, and we'll forget you ever brought it here.

> EVANS shifts the gun to a less threatening position and loosens her grip.

EVANS: I need you to overrule the tenure and promotion committee. And Sherman needs to approve my case. I know how it all works.

JOHNSON: Well . . .

> EVANS points the gun at JOHNSON.

EVANS: You said you were on my side. You said that there was a bad decision. I'm a rising star! You don't deny tenure and promotion to a rising star. I need you to phone Sherman . . . right now. If you overrule the department's decision, he'll go along. He's a huge supporter of my research. Call him. Now! I want this settled. No one is going to take away everything I've worked for.

JOHNSON: OK, OK. I can do this.

> JOHNSON takes out a smartphone or picks up the receiver of his desk phone, and dials.

JOHNSON: Hello, this is Richard Johnson, head of the Department of Therapeutic Genetics. I need to speak to Vice Provost Sherman right away. It will be brief, but it's important . . . Yes . . . That's right, Ms. Blasingame. It's about Nancy Evans' case for tenure and promotion. *(Looks at EVANS in expectation of her approval.)* Yes, Ms. Blasingame.

> EVANS is enraged and points the gun in a more threatening manner at JOHNSON.

EVANS: You've betrayed me. Everyone betrays me. I know what "Ms. Blasingame" means. I took the same security training that you did. That's the code word for a threat by someone with a weapon. You're not helping me with Sherman. When I leave this office, I'll be arrested. You're part of the conspiracy to steal my research.

> EVANS quickly sights the gun.

JOHNSON: No! Please!

> EVANS shoots, and JOHNSON slumps in his chair.

EVANS: Betrayed. By everyone.

> EVANS reaches into her briefcase and pulls out the issue of *University News* with her photograph on the cover. Briefly, she gazes at it with pride. She reads from the cover, full of pride and pleasure.

EVANS: "Rising star in the fight to conquer Alzheimer's" . . . And I looked so pretty!

> EVANS holds the magazine cover directly over her heart and shoots herself through the magazine. She slumps over.

[Scene 6]

> SUZIE DEVEREUX sits in the visitor's chair in THOMAS SHERMAN'S office.

SHERMAN: Thanks for coming right over here.

DEVEREUX: Of course, Tom. I put everything down as soon as I heard about the shootings. I took the service elevator. Some folks might think you should be all broken up and crying, instead of doing your job— protecting the University.

SHERMAN: Good thinking! This is a very awkward business. Very unfortunate. A murder and a suicide. Two faculty members. The shooter was junior faculty. It might appear that Johnson wasn't managing his department properly. Big problems at the department level reflect negatively on me.

DEVEREUX: Maybe this incident would look better as some romantic kind of thing. Just something personal between the two of them. They probably spent a lot of time together in the building. Maybe she wanted him to leave his wife—does he have a wife?—but he refused, and so . . . *(Gestures the motion of shooting a gun.).*

SHERMAN: No. We can't spin it that way. It will come out that Evans had been up for tenure and that the vote went against her. We'll need to play this very well, very carefully. Limit the damage.

DEVEREUX: Of course. That's what I'm here for. But . . . I don't get it. If Nancy Evans was a super-star, why did the tenure vote go against her?

SHERMAN: Sometimes . . . Sometimes, it's easier for a journalist to do a good job when they *don't* know certain things. Certain information . . . complicates the story you want to tell.

DEVEREUX: Yes. I understand.

> DEVEREUX, steps away from SHERMAN and gazes out of the imaginary window. In a moment of introspection and conscience, she delivers a brief soliloquy.

DEVEREUX: I help Sherman tell his lies. Do his dirty schemes. I'm a mouse in his pocket. No, I'm his little scorpian. Is this who I want to be? . . . Well, it's who I am now. Maybe not always.

SHERMAN now looks closely at DEVEREUX. He stands.

SHERMAN: What are you doing over there? Is something wrong?

DEVEREUX turns to face SHERMAN.

DEVEREUX: No. Nothing.

She steps back to SHERMAN and stands close to him.

SHERMAN: I will need to play this very carefully. And you're well positioned to help me.

DEVEREUX: Of course. That's what I'm here for . . . (*Suggestively.*) That . . . and (*Placing an arm on his shoulder.*) maybe more. Maybe what you need right now is a little comfort, a little rejuvenation. After all, Tom, you're under a lot of stress.

SHERMAN takes DEVEREUX'S hand.

SHERMAN: I think you're right. What a smart girl you are, Suzie! My secretary's gone home. There's a little back room in my office suite. You know, for when I need to keep really late hours.

He takes her hand and leads her offstage. As she exits, she pauses, looks back dolefully at the audience, and then follows JOHNSON offstage.

The End

Postscript to "Tenure Denied"

"Tenure Denied" condemns the excesses of the corporate university. Vice Provost for Research Thomas Sherman is corrupt and amoral. He has no regard for the university he serves or for any other human being. Suzie Devereaux is an opportunist and a professional liar. She exhibits moral awareness, but it is displaced by the prospect of professional advancement and the allure of sex with a suave and—more important— powerful person. Richard Johnson is a spineless department chair. Nancy Evans is pathetically self-deluded. We do, however, keenly feel her pain as she plummets from star researcher to failure and outcast for reasons she only barely fathoms. The sense of loss and disillusionment even extends to her feminine vanity as she gazes at the magazine cover:

"Rising star in the fight to conquer Alzheimer's" . . . And I looked so pretty!

This play is loosely based on the life of Dr. Amy Bishop, formerly an assistant professor of biology at the University of Alabama in Huntsville, now serving a life sentence in prison for murdering three members of her department at a faculty meeting shortly after being denied tenure. The play is no defense of Amy Bishop. However, when the shootings occurred back in 2010, I thought that to some extent Bishop was a victim of the PR efforts of the university. The medical device she had invented was not a significant innovation. However, it had been spotlighted by the University president David B Williams as a prime example of why research universities are key to future economic development: "This remarkable technology will change the way biological and medical research is conducted."

> Amy Bishop, UAH biology professor questioned in shooting, is one of university's 'research stars' - al.com

In addition, her research had been hyped in the Huntsville R&D Report, without a careful consideration of its actual value. Her photograph appeared on the cover stating that her "nifty device will rock the cell growth world."

> https://www.nytimes.com/slideshow/2010/02/21/us/0221-
> BISHOP_index/s/0221-BISHOP_slide3.html

The corporate university's desire for self-promotion far outstripped scientific truth, which may well have fed the delusional tendencies of Amy Bishop—as it did the fictional Nancy Evans.

Stripes

A 10-Minute play by

David K. Farkas

Characters:

Professor: He is comically narcissistic, pompous, and arrogant. He's also dishonest and, at moments, cruel.

Student 1: Cowed by the professor.

Student 2: Cowed by the professor.

Graduate Student: Intelligent and resourceful. At times, the graduate student exhibits independent thinking.

Lion

Zebra

Horse

NOTE: The animals should be at least partly costumed. All the animals are intelligent and urbane.

Research Participant 1

Research Participant 2

Offstage Voice at Conference

Suggested Minimum Casting:

Professor

Student 1/ Offstage Voice at Conference

Student 2

Graduate Student

Lion/Fly

Zebra/Horse/ Research Participant 1/Research Participant 2

[Scene 1]

The set suggests a lecture hall. A laptop computer on a table is set up to project PowerPoint slides onto a screen. The professor holds a remote that will begin a presentation and advance the slides. This very unusual remote can also lock and unlock the doors to the lecture hall.

PROF: We are here today to learn why zebras have stripes. Actually, I already know why zebras have stripes, but you don't. *(Rhetorically.)* So, why do zebras have stripes? . . . I am waiting.

Points the remote to the back of the theater (where the audience entered).

PROF: The doors of this lecture hall are now locked. No one can enter or leave. The doors will remain locked until some learning takes place. This is called "instructional design." Now, can someone tell me why zebras have stripes?

STUDENT 1: For camouflage?

PROF: *(With withering ridicule.)* "For camouflage." *(Now condescendingly.)* As men and women of science, let's consider this notion seriously. It is always foolish to reject an explanation without first considering it. Hmmm. We can ask a zebra.

The ZEBRA enters, more or less fully covered in a zebra-striped blanket and a zebra-striped hat.

PROF: *(To ZEBRA.)* Why do zebras have stripes? Is it for camouflage?

ZEBRA: No! Think about it.

The ZEBRA takes the remote from the PROFESSOR and shows a slide of a light brown gazelle well-camouflaged against the light brown of an African savannah. Then the ZEBRA shows a slide of a zebra whose coloring stands out strongly against the light brown of an African savannah.

ZEBRA: Do you want to know how well black-and-white stripes hide zebras from predators?

The LION enters, kills the ZEBRA, and begins eating the ZEBRA in a leisurely manner. The PROFESSOR bends down and gingerly retrieves the remote. He wipes off the ZEBRA'S blood. The LION continues munching on the ZEBRA.

PROF: The answer to the question of why zebras have stripes . . . is definitely not camouflage.

ZEBRA: *(Lying lifeless on the stage.)* I agree.

LION: I agree.

PROF: This is called "survey research." So . . . Why do zebras have stripes?

The LION drags the dead ZEBRA offstage.

STUDENT 2: Because stripes align the life forces of the zebra with the natural balance of the universe?

PROF: Love this answer! "Align the life forces." "Natural balance of the universe." This is called "theory." What's really good about theory is that it can never be tested, never be proven true or false. Therefore, we can assume it's true. Very convenient. You can ask acupuncturists about "energy flow" . . . As it happens, I myself have done some work in this area.

Shows a slide of the acupuncture zones of a zebra. STUDENT 2 takes notes and continues to do so from time to time.

PROF: Wait, you haven't seen the best part.

The PROFESSOR beckons offstage. The LION re-enters, dragging the bloody carcass of the ZEBRA. Patches of red cloth taped loosely to the ZEBRA suggest the blood stains. The LION exits. Now the PROFESSOR sticks two extra-large pins into one of the ZEBRA'S ears. The ZEBRA returns to a healthy, energetic appearance and pulls off the red patches.

ZEBRA: I feel better already.

The PROFESSOR turns to the audience.

PROF: I would say that some applause is in order!

The PROFESSOR gestures insistently for applause from the students and from the theater audience. STUDENT 1, STUDENT 2, and the audience applaud.

PROF: Now, let's return to our topic for today. Why do zebras have stripes?

The FLY, formerly the LION, enters.

FLY: You need to get your answer from the folks with their "boots on the ground"— or, in this case, "wings in the air"—which would be me.

The FLY takes the remote and displays a slide that seems to show the hide of a zebra.

FLY: Zebras have thinner hides than other African mammals. Therefore, they are especially vulnerable to flies. This is very nice if you are a fly. But, unfortunately, evolution is full of sneaky tricks, and zebras gradually developed a pattern of irregular black and white stripes because this confuses the visual system of flies. When we try to bite a zebra, we very often fail to land or crash land and bounce off. Let me demonstrate.

The FLY makes repeated unsuccessful attempts to land on the ZEBRA.

ZEBRA: Because our skin is so thin, confusing the visual system of flies is more important to us than getting eaten by lions.

PROF: This makes perfect sense. We call this "formal logic." Clearly it is much better to be eaten by a lion than bitten by a fly.

The FLY makes more unsuccessful attempts to land on the ZEBRA, gives up in frustration and exits.

GRAD STUDENT: I think I need more evidence.

PROF: You want "more evidence"? This is why I don't normally allow graduate students to register for my undergraduate courses. However, I do see an opportunity for Federal research funding, and therefore I am willing to consider the possibility of conducting empirical research. Let's see . . . We will need two zebras. One will be an ordinary zebra with ordinary stripes. We call this zebra "the control"—and, as a fun name, "Sammy."

ZEBRA: OK, I'm "Sammy."

PROF: And we will need one zebra without stripes. We will call this zebra "the independent variable." . . . Yes . . . Yes . . . That will work. When theory or when formal logic fails—and, by the way, "fails" means doesn't get funded, we resort to the scientific method. *(Pause.)* So, where were we? Yes . . . *(To GRAD STUDENT.)* Get me a stripeless zebra. It needs to be identical to Sammy, except, of course, for the stripes. It needs to be the same height, the same weight, and the same age as Sammy. Also, the same level of education. We don't want any uncontrolled variables.

GRAD STUDENT: Yes, Professor.

PROF: We're on a tight schedule. I'm hoping to get a publication or two out of this—high impact, archival journals, of course. So, I need you to get me that "Plain Jane" stripeless zebra by Monday. You shouldn't have any trouble getting a Plain Jane zebra. *(To audience.)* This is called "mentoring your graduate students." By the way, the phrase "Plain Jane zebra" is an instance of the sexism endemic to modern science—we need to do something about this.

[Scene 2]

The scene is still the lecture hall. Only the PROFESSOR and the GRAD STUDENT are onstage.

GRAD STUDENT: Professor, I was unable to obtain a stripeless zebra with the exact same height, weight, age, and level of education as "Sammy." Actually, I was unable to obtain any stripeless zebra at all. All the zebras I could obtain for our experiment look a lot like Sammy. By the way, I think I was told back in high school: Never name your laboratory zebras. That can make you feel very sad later on. You know, if we have to euthanize Sammy.

ZEBRA: *(Offstage).* What!? Euthanize me!

PROF: *(Pondering.)* Euthanize Sammy? . . . We'll cross that bridge when we come to it.

GRAD STUDENT: I did think up an alternative research design. As everyone here knows, this play is being performed in Swampington Marsh, South Carolina, famous for aggressive flies.

PROF: This is called "suspension of disbelief"—fundamental to the scientific method. Because we are right now in a swampy, fly-infested horse pasture . . .

A slide of a horse pasture displays automatically.

PROF: . . . we have a horse—plagued by flies.

> The HORSE, formerly the ZEBRA, dressed in dark brown, enters twitching and, if possible, shaking its tail to try to ward off flies.

PROF: This horse is very unhappy, because South Carolina flies, unable to find zebras, their preferred food source, make life utterly miserable for horses. *(Turning to the HORSE.)* Would you agree?

HORSE: Neigh.

PROF: The horse may have said "Nay," but we'll record the answer as a "yes." Again, "survey research."

> Someone steps onstage to hand the GRAD STUDENT the zebra-striped blanket, now folded so that it will only cover half of the HORSE.

GRAD STUDENT: So, we cover half of the body of this horse with this specially fabricated zebra suit . . .

> Wraps the zebra-striped blanket around the HORSE, but just from the waist down. The HORSE is now half-covered, and the GRAD STUDENT steps back.

GRAD STUDENT: . . . and we observe what happens.

PROF: This is called "observational research."

> The FLY enters and tries to land on the bottom half of the HORSE, but in repeated, and comic, attempts either misses or bounces off.

HORSE: Hey, this is great.

> The FLY now turns to the top half of the HORSE and bites multiple times.

HORSE: Not so great.

> The HORSE slides the zebra suit around from top to bottom and from bottom to top trying to fully protect itself, but the FLY always finds the unprotected half of the HORSE.

PROF: We are conducting multiple trials to get "robust" data. We are hoping to approach—but not obtain—statistical significance. If our results are statistically insignificant, we can ask for more funding. We *should* be recording the number of bites on the protected and unprotected regions of the horse, controlling for surface area and the educational level of each region of the horse.

> At the phrase "educational level of each region of the horse," the HORSE looks at the PROFESSOR as though the PROFESSOR is crazy. The other animals gesture in agreement with the HORSE.

But I forgot to include this numerical stuff in my research design, so we'll have to "ballpark" it. This is called "ballpark research." It works pretty well if you know how to write up your research findings. This is the kind of thing we teach our graduate students.

> The FLY steps back, seemingly satisfied from drawing blood from the HORSE.

FLY: I don't need to be greedy. I'll return at dinner time.

HORSE: This is a high-priority research area from the perspective of the equine world.

OFFSTAGE VOICE AT CONFERENCE: *(As the PROFESSOR basks in imagined acclaim.)* I am very honored to introduce our keynote conference speaker!

> The PROFESSOR snaps out of his reverie and proudly casts a sweeping glance across his very large imagined audience. Then he returns to the classroom.

PROF: Now comes the really important part. Once we did science to learn about nature, to unlock the secrets of the Universe, and to contribute to the betterment of Humankind. Now, we do science to obtain funding and to become entrepreneurs who start companies. Even the Horse knows about this.

> The HORSE nods.

FLY: Even I know about that.

> The FLY exits.

PROF: That's why the University funds my lab. They get a cut of all of my research funding and a much bigger cut if I can commercialize my research. This is how big universities operate nowadays. I've been working with a few of my colleagues in the English department on a "Chaucer lab." We haven't gotten too far yet. But they know how important this is for the future of their department. *(Addressing the audience very directly.)* Class, do you have any ideas about commercializing this research on zebra stripes? Think hard. *(Gestures with the remote and then turns ominous.)* You do want to go home tonight—don't you?

GRAD STUDENT: How about this? Zebra-striped clothing as a healthier alternative to DEET and those other nasty insect repellents?

PROF: *(Completely surprised.)* Yes! Yes! Yes! Very good. Here's our start-up! One moment. Before we go any further, I need you to sign this.

The GRAD STUDENT signs.

PROF: Your idea now belongs to me. *(To audience.)* This is called "informed consent"—very important.

The LION enters.

LION: I want to invest. Lions, as a species, are wealthy. We have "deep pockets." Not as deep as kangaroos, but deep enough for us to have a seat at the table. We are *(The LION growls.)* the real predators on Wall Street.

GRAD STUDENT: This is called "private placement." The general public doesn't get to invest in the really promising start-ups. Just a coterie of billionaires and a few privileged species—the 1% of the animal kingdom.

PROF: Now comes the crucial phase of our research. Confirming that we can monetize our findings. The results will determine whether my lab will continue to be funded. Also, whether I get to buy a lovely summer home in Maine and, perhaps, a villa in Tuscany. Quite a lot is hanging in the balance.

[Scene 3]

Stagehands enter with a table and may otherwise change the set from a classroom to some kind of research lab.

PROF: Now we see what happens, what my idea is really worth.

On the table is a large bottle of liquid labeled "Nasty bug repellent (You don't want this)." Next to the bottle is a big sign reading "Much Better Alternative," with a large arrow pointing away from the table.

The GRAD STUDENT enters modeling a zebra-striped T-shirt and stands where the arrow points.

PROF: This is called "unbiased research." Now comes the big moment.

RESEARCH PARTICIPANT 1 enters, goes directly to the table. RESEARCH PARTICIPANT 1 carefully examines the bottle, reads the sign, approaches the GRAD STUDENT with the zebra-striped T-shirt, and becomes seriously disoriented.

RESEARCH PARTICIPANT 1: Arrh! My visual system is confused! I am nauseous. What a terrible user experience.

RESEARCH PARTICIPANT 1 exits with difficulty and returns immediately with a minor costume change to become RESEARCH PARTICIPANT 2. RESEARCH PARTICIPANT 2 goes to the table, examines the bottle, and then turns to the sign, seemingly with enthusiasm. Following the sign, RESEARCH PARTICIPANT 2 approaches the GRAD STUDENT with the zebra-striped T-shirt but becomes seriously disoriented.

RESEARCH PARTICIPANT 2: Arrh! My aesthetic system is confused—and grossed out. I'm sick. Who would wear such an ugly thing! Give me my DEET!

RESEARCH PARTICIPANT 2 exits to return soon as the HORSE. The LION slips back onstage.

PROF: *(Insistently.)* There is still value to my idea! Those subjects were . . . were . . . "outliers."

LION and GRAD STUDENT: No, they were not.

The HORSE enters with the zebra blanket wrapped around his bottom half.

HORSE: *(To GRAD STUDENT.)* If no human being is going to walk around in a zebra striped T-shirt, may I have it?

The GRAD STUDENT removes the T-shirt and puts it on the top half of the HORSE so that the HORSE is more or less covered in zebra stripes.

GRAD STUDENT: This is called "ethical research."

HORSE: *(Pointing to himself.)* This is called "a happy horse."

Actors freeze. Changes are made mid-scene so that we are back in a classroom setting. STUDENT 1 and STUDENT 2 enter and take their seats. Action resumes.

PROF: Our lecture is finished. You may all leave . . . provided that I receive applause for my outstanding lecture.

The LION and the GRADUATE STUDENT offer tepid applause.

PROF: You can do better than that.

The LION and the GRADUATE STUDENT feign more enthusiastic applause.

PROF: *(To LION and GRADUATE STUDENT.)* That will suffice. *(To theater audience.)* This is called "sound pedagogy." The louder you can get your students to applaud, the more they have learned. Read B. F. Skinner on this.

The PROFESSOR raises and clicks the remote.

PROF: The doors of the lecture hall are now unlocked. You may all leave. The LION and GRADUATE student bolt for the exit.

HORSE: *(Holding up Tim Caro's book.)* To learn all about zebra stripe research—very good research—read Tim Caro's book, *Zebra Stripes.*

The End

Postscript to "Stripes"

"Stripes" is both a fantastical story, full of comic silliness, and a harsh satire. The Professor has absorbed the pernicious values of the corporate university with its focus on funding and the commercialization of research. To climb the academic ladder and to pursue great wealth, he makes mincemeat of the scientific method and research ethics. The Professor is also, for very obvious reasons, a terrible instructor. Furthermore, he steals the Graduate Student's idea for commercializing the zebra stripe research.

As in many stories with both humans and talking animals, the Zebra, the Lion, the Horse, and the Fly are smart and truthful. As in many satires, there is a tip-off passage where the satirist's values (often in their most extreme form) are openly displayed:

> **PROFESSOR:** Once we did science to learn about nature, to unlock the secrets of the Universe, and to contribute to the betterment of Humankind. Now, we do science to obtain funding and to become entrepreneurs who start companies . . .
>
> I've been working with a few of my colleagues in the English department on a "Chaucer lab." We haven't gotten too far yet. But they know how important this is for the future of their department.

The idea of a "Chaucer lab" is ridiculous, an instance of a humanities department turning itself inside out in order to conform to the monetary demands of the corporate university. But the play does have a happy ending: The Horse gets to keep the striped blanket and T-shirt.

The Special Status of Clara de Jong

A 10-minute play by

David K. Farkas

Characters:

Provost Stanley Banfield

Professor Elaine Elko: Chair of the English Department.

Professor Clara de Jong

Professor Rick Cardoza

Professor Tom Schwartz

Professor Lionel Fitzpatrick: An older man.

Suggested minimum casting:

Elaine Elko

Clara de Jong

Provost Banfield/Lionel Fitzpatrick (with a quick costume change)

Rick Cardoza/Tom Schwartz (with a quick costume change)

[Scene 1]

> PROFESSOR ELAINE ELKO, chair of the English department, is seated in the visitor's chair in the very comfortable office of PROVOST STANLEY BANFIELD. Her posture is stiff. BANFIELD sits behind his desk.

PROVOST BANFIELD: You are aware that your department is out of compliance with Phase 2 of the University's faculty diversity initiative.

ELAINE: Yes, of course I am.

PROVOST BANFIELD: You have ten full-time faculty. Phase 1 called for 10% representation from marginalized populations, and you were in compliance. You had one faculty who identified as marginalized. Now, with Phase 2 kicking in, the target is 20%. But this year you have no—zero—marginalized faculty. As other departments improve, English is getting worse. You can't get any worse than zero percent. You don't look good. I don't look good. President McCabe doesn't look good. There will be consequences. What happened anyway?

ELAINE: Nothing really happened at all.

PROVOST BANFIELD: Did someone quit? Is your department unwelcoming to people of color, hostile to gender minorities?

ELAINE: No. Nothing like that. Our marginalized faculty member is Clara de Jong. She is one-fourth Black. Some years she lists herself as Black. Some years she doesn't. This year she didn't. The actual ethnic composition of the faculty hasn't changed at all.

PROVOST BANFIELD: She can't make up her mind?

ELAINE: I wouldn't put it that way. She does make up her mind. Various personal factors seem to determine how Black she feels at any given time.

PROVOST BANFIELD: This is a very unfortunate situation.

ELAINE: We haven't had a new faculty line in a decade. If you gave us a new position, we would hire someone to teach courses in Black literature. A lot of students want to study Black writers as well as writers from other groups that English departments have neglected. You know that I ask and ask, and I argue our case. But I never get that line.

PROVOST BANFIELD: Everyone asks for new positions.

ELAINE: Yes, but how many departments haven't gotten one in a decade?

PROVOST BANFIELD: Why doesn't Clara de Jong teach courses in Black literature? She considers herself black some of the time. That should qualify her.

ELAINE: No, it does not. Her fields are Restoration Comedy and the nineteenth century British novel. She has no special qualifications to teach courses in Black literature. She doesn't *want* to teach Black literature.

PROVOST BANFIELD: What about other members of the Department?

ELAINE: There are people who know something about the area, but White faculty are apprehensive about teaching a course in Black literature. They think—and they may be right—that students expect a Black instructor. If we had the new position, we could at least reach the 10% mark. If Clara self-identified as Black, we'd be at 20%, and we'd meet the Phase 2 target.

PROVOST BANFIELD: Not quite. Your math is off.

ELAINE: What?

PROVOST BANFIELD: If you had a new faculty line, you'd have 11 faculty. So, one faculty from a marginalized population would give the department 9%, and two faculty would only give 18%, not 20%. But that should be close enough, at least for the near term. You need to work with de Jong. Put a little pressure on her.

ELAINE: I'm not going to "put pressure" on her, and you have no business suggesting that I do.

PROVOST BANFIELD: Then you have a problem. Don't expect a new position. Your focus should be returning to the 10% level. Prove you're not hostile to marginalized groups before we think about any new position.

ELAINE: We're not at all hostile. Clara de Jong is very happy in our department.

PROVOST BANFIELD: Elaine, this is your problem. Deal with it. Just so you know, my budget is tight, and I'm not likely to approve any sabbatical applications from English. Connecting your offices to the new campus wifi? Won't happen soon.

ELAINE: Totally unfair, Stanley.

ELAINE exits angrily.

[Scene 2]

CLARA, carrying some books, strolls across the stage. She looks White, although she should not be notably light skinned. PROFESSOR RICK CARDOZA enters and approaches CLARA. Both are dressed in clothing that suggests warm weather.

RICK CARDOZA: Hi, Clara.

CLARA: Hi, Rick.

RICK CARDOZA: Hey, Clara. Louise and I are having some folks over to our place on the fifteenth—a week from this Saturday. We're doing a Southern-style bar-be-que. Can you make it?

CLARA: "Southern-style bar-be-que"? That sounds like something new for you folks.

RICK CARDOZA: Well, yes. But, you know. Louise loves to be creative with her cooking.

CLARA DE: Sure, I can join you. Thanks. I'm a vegetarian, so I'll bring a veggie patty. It should cook up just fine on your bar-be-que.

RICK, caught by surprise, is momentarily flustered.

RICK CARDOZA: Sure, Louise's Southern-style bar-be-que sauce will go great with veggie patties.

CLARA: Yeah. I think so.

RICK CARDOZA: Come by around 6:00. We'll eat indoors if it's rainy.

CLARA: OK, sure. Thanks.

RICK CARDOZA exits as CLARA watches him with a bemused look on her face. TOM SCHWARTZ enters wearing earbuds. He walks with some rhythm in his step, as though responding to the beat of music. He stops as he reaches CLARA.

TOM SCHWARTZ: Hiya, Clara!

CLARA gives a big nod because she knows that a verbal greeting will not be heard. TOM removes the ear buds.

TOM SCHWARTZ: Just listening to that Motown sound—Four Tops. Love that stuff. What about you?

CLARA: Sure, I like Motown. I like lots of kinds of music—especially Broadway show tunes.

TOM SCHWARTZ: Like, Porgy and Bess? Dreamgirls?

CLARA: *(Showing annoyance.)* All kinds of Broadway shows.

TOM SCHWARTZ: Got it! Catch you later.

TOM exits with a bit of uncertainty in his manner. CLARA stands watching him with an irritated look on her face. ELAINE ELKO enters. CLARA approaches ELAINE ready to speak.

ELAINE: What is it, Clara?

CLARA: Elaine, are you about to say something calculated to re-awaken my Blackness? Start a conversation about singing in church or cornrow braids? I'd appreciate it if you didn't.

ELAINE: No. Certainly not.

CLARA: But you do know what I'm talking about.

ELAINE: You might say I have a good guess. The faculty all know we're being screwed because we're out of compliance with the diversity initiative.

CLARA: The only logical solution is to give us a new position—someone to teach Black literature and help with diversity compliance.

ELAINE: But we're not going to get that new position *because* we're out of compliance.

CLARA: That's like a Catch 22!

ELAINE: Yup.

CLARA: Well, I'm not going to be pressured. My feelings about my ethnic background are deeply personal. And my colleagues should know my family is Dutch. There's no Motown, no gospel music, and no collard greens in my family background. My paternal grandfather lived in Cape Town and married an African woman. My parents were raised in Haarlem—that's "Haarlem" with two "A"s. It's about a 20-minute train ride from Amsterdam.

ELAINE: Well, I'm not going to say anything to anyone in the department about your background. That's for you to do, if you want to do it. I'm certainly not defending Rick and Tom. But what they are hoping for is understandable. You list yourself as Black most years. They just wish you'd go the whole distance toward being Black.

CLARA: Well, we'll see. I don't owe the department anything.

ELAINE: That's true. You need to think about your own sense of personal identity—not the department's problems.

They exit in opposite directions.

[Scene 3]

CLARA is seated, perhaps at a coffee-shop table, with PROFESSOR LIONEL FITZPATRICK.

CLARA: Lionel! Early retirement. I had no idea.

PROFESSOR FITZPATRICK: It's not what I want. I'm 62 and figured on going to age 66—to get my full social security. I know I have four more years of good teaching in me. But the Department really needs a new hire, and it doesn't look like we'll get a new faculty line. So, I'm willing to make room for a new person.

CLARA: You're thinking that the new position would be a minority hire, help us meet the University's diversity goals?

PROFESSOR FITZPATRICK: Yes.

CLARA: But do we even know we'd keep your line? The provost can take it back if he wants.

PROFESSOR FITZPATRICK: Well, that would be Elaine's battle to fight. I can only do what I can do.

CLARA: But Elaine loses more often than she wins. Banfield's such a prick.

PROFESSOR FITZPATRICK: Well, the situation isn't promising for any humanities department when the provost comes out of the business school. I think Banfield's area is accounting,

CLARA: It would really hurt you to retire now, wouldn't it Lionel?

PROFESSOR FITZPATRICK: Yes, it would be a bit tough financially. And I don't want to give up teaching. But I've had a long and happy career here, and I feel an obligation to serve the interests of the Department.

CLARA: *(Deeply moved.)* I see.

They exit as actors.

[Scene 4]

PROFESSOR ELAINE ELKO is seated in the visitor's chair in Provost Banfield's office.

ELAINE: So here's what I'm offering. Clara de Jong will permanently self-identify as Black. I have her commitment on that. Professor Fitzpatrick promises to retire in four years. In return, you give us a budget line right now to hire a tenure track assistant professor to teach Black literature. So, this costs you an assistant professor's salary for four years. Then, you get Fitzpatrick's line back. I'll fight like hell to keep it, but we'll leave that for the future. If we get the new hire in Black literature and with Clara's commitment, our compliance will reach 18%—close enough, as you said. I understand that you accountants call that "rounding up."

PROVOST BANFIELD: I can see some value here. Can I count on Fitzpatrick and de Jong following through?

ELAINE: Without a doubt. Our faculty live up to their commitments. Of course, you need to live up to yours. Do we have a deal? You'll look good. President McCabe will look good. The University will look good. You know, Lionel is a very healthy, very energetic guy. It wasn't easy for me to get his agreement on this. If we don't get this deal done, he'll probably teach till he's 80—and he gets that full professor salary.

PROVOST BANFIELD: We have a deal. You get the Black literature position.

ELAINE: Excellent!

PROVOST BANFIELD: But remember, you're still at 18%—almost in compliance, but not quite. There are still areas where I'm going to favor the departments that are fully in compliance.

ELAINE: But you said that 18% was "close enough."

PROVOST BANFIELD: Well, close enough for some things. But not for everything. I'll decide on a case-by-case basis whether English will be penalized for not having achieved full compliance. Eighteen percent is not twenty percent.

ELKO stands and speaks angrily.

ELAINE: No! I'm not going to get fucked over again, Stanley . . . I've been a faculty member here for 23 years, and I have friends. I know things. There are some ambiguous sections in the faculty handbook, and I'll use them. Do you really want to go to war against me? I'm an honest person, an ethical person, but maybe not when I've been pushed past the limit.

PROVOST BANFIELD: Ha! You're bluffing, Elaine. But I'll say this much. You're talking a language I understand.

ELAINE: You don't think I can't create some serious headaches for you? Think about it. Maybe it's better for us to be friends.

PROVOST BANFIELD pauses to think and then smiles.

PROVOST BANFIELD: Well, maybe the English department should be applauded for moving up from zero to 18%. Achievements should always be recognized.

ELAINE: I do appreciate that, Stanley. I'll write you a letter of understanding about Clara and about Lionel. You write one giving us the new position and congratulating us on our rapid progress toward full compliance. No, I want your letter to state that we have achieved "interim full compliance" and that is completely acceptable to you.

PROVOST BANFIELD: OK, we have a deal. I'll write that letter. And you will tell your faculty that English always has my strong support.

ELAINE: When they get the good news about the new position, they'll know you're doing your best for us.

PROVOST BANFIELD: Things may be looking up for the English department. You're learning how to get things done around here. It's all about negotiation, being tough, using your leverage. If you required your English majors to take a few courses in the business school, they'd go through life a lot sharper and a lot tougher.

ELAINE: You don't need to take business courses to know when you're dealing with people who need to be pushed into doing what's right. Our students read texts that expand their minds, and that's excellent preparation for the future—any possible future that comes their way. Your business students need more of what *we* teach.

PROVOST BANFIELD: "Expand their minds"—that's just your standard humanities bullshit that no one believes any more. You folks are so pompous. You love to take the high ground. But once you scratch the surface, universities are just part the business world.

ELAINE: No! Universities are something different. Our value to society comes in large part because we are *not* the business world.

PROVOST BANFIELD: Of course. Of course . . . You know, my job is keeping this university running. President McCabe and I will both benefit from your "interim full compliance," and it's not going to cost me a whole lot of money. From my point of view, this meeting has been a good return on 15 minutes of my time. Now, Elaine, if you'll excuse me. I need to get on to the next thing on my schedule.

ELAINE: Sure enough. It's always a pleasure, Stanley.

The End

Postscript to "The Special Status of Clara de Jong"

This play strongly expresses two themes that have appeared in this collection of plays: Faculty autonomy and the value of a humanities education. When Provost Banfield tells Elaine to pressure Clara into declaring herself Black, Elaine refuses. Clara will make her own decisions. When Banfield belittles the humanities, Elaine responds forcefully.

Furthermore, this play concludes the collection on a positive note: Score one for the good guys. Because Provost Banfield is narrow-minded and unscrupulous, we do not mind that Elaine Elko lies to Banfield when she says that Lionel Fitzpatrick intended to keep teaching (and earn his relatively high full professor salary) until he is 80.

The new elements in this play are the tricky issues of racial identity and the challenge of achieving diversity in academia. The plot largely turns on the special circumstance that Clara de Jong, being one-fourth African, can very reasonably choose whether or not to declare herself Black. I know of an academic department in which the chair each year implored a one-quarter Black faculty member to self-identify as Black, so as to raise the department's diversity score. However, because ethnicity is a complex part of anyone's personality, this individual periodically changed their mind.

I take the university's faculty diversity initiative as a good thing, although, as is true of so many policies and requirements in large organizations, it is a blunt instrument that does not necessarily apply well to particular situations. Here we see it weaponized against the English department by an unsympathetic administrator.

The attempts by Pat Cardoza and Tom Schwartz to influence Clara to classify herself as Black, while well-intentioned, are clumsy, and understandably annoy Clara. Clara finally makes her own choice, prompted by Lionel Fitzpatrick's act of self-sacrifice. In this respect, Clara is like Eric Sloane in "Quality Work." She will not be bossed around by anyone, but she is willing to make a change for the greater good.

Although the issue is often contested, my view is that a White person can teach Black literature (or sing the blues). But to keep the play's themes and concerns straightforward, I finessed this issue with the circumstance that the students referred to in the play want to be taught Black literature by a Black person and that the English department faculty, including Clara de Jong herself, do not want to teach Black literature.

Writing the 10-Minute Play

Ten-minute plays are surprisingly quick and easy to write. In contrast to the short story and novel, you don't have to think about the complexities of managing a narrative voice—first person, third person, ironic, omniscient, less-than-omniscient, etc. Essentially, you think of a story that will serve as a plot, and you write the dialogue for your characters. There is minimal descriptive writing. You write stage directions, but this is just bare-bones writing that a theater audience will never see.

Coming up with a plot is the biggest challenge. But the brevity of the 10-minute play enforces a relatively simple plot. You are not coordinating plots with subplots. You're not likely to have more than five characters. You may well have just two or three.

A good plan is to start with a part of the world you know well—for instance, the legal profession if you are an attorney. Then you think through the notable events you have experienced or heard about, looking for those that intrigue you and seem to have dramatic possibilities. When you choose an intriguing situation, do not be tied down to what actually happened. Exaggerate, go further. Take the story in an entirely different direction. One playwriting precept—and a good one—is "raise the stakes." In other words, the situation in the play needs to be highly consequential. If the intriguing event that occurred in your law firm resulted in someone getting reprimanded, be very willing to get them fired. Or sent to jail.

Your plot may have nothing to do with the events of your life or things you have seen happen. Your play might be historical or might come from a news story. It may come from your daydreams and fantasies, which you may need to clean up for public consumption.

I often look for situations that have an instability—situations in which, for one reason or another, there will need to be a change or in which a change is likely and plausible. Then I look for a way to resolve the instability that is impactful and, ideally, surprising. For example, in "The Day of the Deal," the initial instability is that Walter and Ruth's relationship seems destined to end, with Walter enjoying professional success and Ruth finding only disappointment. This instability becomes a crisis when Ruth is cruelly deceived at the conference and then confesses her infidelity. The resolution—Walter's forgiveness of Ruth—comes with two surprises: Ruth, not Walter, will get to edit the medieval manuscript and (in a humorous vein) Ruth will agree to adopt Walter's affluent lifestyle.

"The Day of the Deal" is about two people in a relationship, but many 10-minute plays are built around one main character (the protagonist), and that character may be you—probably in some disguised form. Whatever the number of main characters, each should have a goal—something they want (even if this is just to be left alone). You may also want to give your main characters different value systems. These differing goals and values are likely to lead to a conflict, and this conflict will need to be resolved in some way.

There are 10-minute plays in which the plot turns entirely on events or facts that are revealed as the characters talk to each other. Perhaps long-hidden secrets are revealed during a family gathering. It is best, however, if the plot also includes new events that take place (even if they take place offstage) during the time period dramatized in the play. There are many, many websites and books that fully explain these and other sound playwriting precepts. But feel free to ignore any precept and go your own way.

Ten-minute plays are regularly staged by community theaters, usually in 10-minute play "festivals" consisting of seven or eight plays performed together in rapid succession. Many community theaters invite playwrights to submit their scripts for consideration (often with a submission fee). Community theaters almost always specify a maximum cast size, perhaps four or five actors. Sets must be very simple because each set must be put in place and taken down very quickly. Many festivals are strict about the 10-minute running time (or maximum page length of the submitted script). Others are flexible. As I noted (in the postscript to "Graduation"), you can easily round up some friends to perform one or more 10-minute plays, most likely script-in-hand. Doing so is great fun and short-circuits the submission process.

Whether you are submitting a play to a festival or performing it yourself, some plot ideas are not feasible because they present daunting staging difficulties. Naval battles are tough. But there are many ways to make your play's setting less realistic and therefore easier to stage. For example, in "Paradise in Tennessee," which is set in 1971, there is a brief scene in which Professor Rogers phones his wife from a pay phone. Although it would not be very difficult to build an imitation payphone and receiver, the actor can simply pantomime the phone call. The 10-minute play "Horizons," which is included in *Performing 10-Minute Plays with Friends,* depicts a ground-crew employee who has flown off in a commercial airliner and two jet fighter pilots who are pursuing him. The actors "fly their planes" sitting on ordinary chairs. Finally, you can shift gears and write a "radio play" that is intended only to be read.

Most 10-minute plays consist of a single scene. A smaller number have a second scene, often a short scene that functions as a kind of coda. Ten-minute plays consisting of three or four scenes are, broadly speaking, frowned upon in the theater world. Rejecting standard practice, I am comfortable writing and staging 10-minute plays consisting of four, five, or more scenes. The benefit is that you can tell a bigger story. The drawback is that to retain momentum, scene transitions must be quick and smooth, often through the use of split sets. Another useful technique for accelerating the action is to write scenes in which the actors withdraw to the periphery of the stage but do not actually exit. Using these techniques, the very informal Goat Hill Theater effectively staged (in the Farkas family living room) "Professor Jim," with its 11 short scenes. The running time was about 14 minutes. Although I strongly believe that multi-scene 10-minute plays can work well, you should know that community theaters are apt to reject such scripts.

Domain-focused collections

You might consider writing a collection of domain-focused 10-minute plays—like this collection of academic plays. By "domain," I mean some part of the world or some theme or issue. The legal profession is a domain, so is old age or the special problems faced by transgender people. If you start writing 10-minute plays, a domain-focused collection may take shape little by little without any planning on your part. It is natural for people to write repeatedly about a domain they know well. You can even use some of the same characters from one play to the next. I was surprised when I realized that a significant number of my 10-minute plays derived in one way or another from my background as a Jew. Once I decided on a Jewish-focused collection, I set about writing more Jewish plays—some highly personal, some not personal at all. Because I enjoyed creating *Fourteen Jewish Flavored 10-Minute Plays,* I followed it up with the present collection.

Finally, if you put together a collection of 10-minute plays, you should consider what extra components you may want to add. There should at least be an introduction. Extra components provide context and depth. Readers who like a play may well be interested in learning how the play originated and what you were trying to say and achieve. You can also point out, as I have done, significant relationships among the plays.

www.ingramcontent.com/pod-product-compliance
Lightning Source LLC
Chambersburg PA
CBHW051137020726
47501CB00005B/1553